"Why do you have this silly idea I'm a nanny?"

Susan asked dismally.

"It's not silly," Dean said at last. "I'm being perfectly rational."

"You're always very rational. But, in this case, you're also being silly."

"But I'm not! Susan, think carefully. Do you remember being my wife? Do you remember anything at all?"

"I don't remember much of anything because my head feels pretty muddled," she said defiantly. "But the doctor said that's perfectly understandable. It will all come back."

"Susan, what do you remember about our marriage, about us?"

"I remember a lot, a lot that a nanny wouldn't remember. Intimate things. Bedroom things. You and me things. Not just nanny things. You take me upstairs to that bedroom and I'll prove to you once and for all that I'm your wife. I'll prove to you that I remember the most important things about being your wife...."

Dear Reader,

This July, Silhouette Romance cordially invites you to a month of marriage stories, based upon *your* favorite themes. There's no need to RSVP; just pick up a book, start reading...and be swept away by romance.

The month kicks off with our Fabulous Fathers title, *And Baby Makes Six*, by talented author Pamela Dalton. Two single parents marry for convenience' sake, only to be surprised to learn they're expecting a baby of their own!

In Natalie Patrick's *Three Kids and a Cowboy*, a woman agrees to stay married to her husband just until he adopts three adorable orphans, but soon finds herself longing to make the arrangement permanent. And the romance continues when a beautiful wedding consultant asks her sexy neighbor to pose as her fiancé in *Just Say I Do* by RITA Award-winning author Lauryn Chandler.

The reasons for weddings keep coming, with a warmly humorous story of amnesia in Vivian Leiber's *The Bewildered Wife;* a new take on the runaway bride theme in *Have Honeymoon, Need Husband* by Robin Wells; and a green card wedding from debut author Elizabeth Harbison in *A Groom for Maggie.*

Here's to your reading enjoyment!

Melissa Senate
Senior Editor
Silhouette Romance

Please address questions and book requests to:
Silhouette Reader Service
U.S.: 3010 Walden Ave., P.O. Box 1325, Buffalo, NY 14269
Canadian: P.O. Box 609, Fort Erie, Ont. L2A 5X3

THE BEWILDERED WIFE

Vivian Leiber

Silhouette
ROMANCE™
Published by Silhouette Books
America's Publisher of Contemporary Romance

For my husband, who taught me that lightning really
does strike twice.

 SILHOUETTE BOOKS

ISBN 0-373-19237-1

THE BEWILDERED WIFE

Copyright © 1997 by Arlynn Leiber Presser

VIVIAN LEIBER's

writing talent runs in the family. Her great-grandmother wrote a popular collection of Civil War-era poetry, her grandfather Fritz was an award-winning science-fiction writer and her father still writes science fiction and fantasy today. Vivian hopes that her two sons follow the family tradition, but so far the five-year-old's ambition is to be a construction worker and own a toy store, while her other boy wants to be a truck driver.

5 Reasons why the nanny should keep thinking she's our MOM— and DAD's Wife!

(By the Radcliffe children, Chelsea, Henry and Baby Edward)

1) Susan tells the best bed time stories—even if dad thinks it's all a bunch of nonsense.

2) She doesn't have a family of her own, so we should share ours with her.

3) She saved our dog during the scary lightening storm.

4) We like her better than all our other nannies.

5) Even though daddy tries to keep it a secret, we see him kissing her ALL the time!

Chapter One

"Susan, make a wish," Chelsea begged.

Susan looked around the dining room table. Chelsea, Henry and Baby Edward's faces were lit by excitement and by the twelve candles on a chocolate cake—Chelsea had run out of both candles and patience long before she could spear the cake with all twenty-seven.

"Come on, make a wish," Henry demanded. He was dressed in Batman pajama bottoms, but had decided to wrap the matching top around his head like a turban. A tube that had been used to mail architectural drawings to his father was shoved into his waistband—ready to draw, to strike, at the first sign of trouble.

Susan took a deep breath.

I wish…I wish all this were mine, she thought. And then immediately chastised herself.

It wasn't hers, could never be hers, and it was very selfish to want it.

But it wasn't the Radcliffe mansion, the forty-acre grounds, the luxury cars or the Radcliffe collection of late-nineteenth-century American painters she longed for. She didn't pine for the jewels locked away in a safe behind a panel in the upstairs library. She wouldn't even want the heavy Queen Anne furniture, the soft Aubusson rugs or the ornate silver flatware that lay dusty and tarnished in the beveled-glass cabinets of the butler's pantry.

No, she wasn't wishing for any of the expensive and elegant things that made the Radcliffe family one of the wealthiest in the country.

It was other things she wished for, intangible things that couldn't be measured by an accountant or valued on a bank statement.

Things that she hesitated to name, even in silence, even before her birthday cake, which glittered more brightly than gold on the dining room table.

It was out of the question that her wishes would be granted, presumptuous even to blow out the candles with these thoughts on her mind.

Out of reach for a nanny who was paid well above minimum wage but still not enough to afford even a single fork on the table before her. Out of reach for a woman who, at twenty-seven, had no husband or child or even a home to call her own.

Still, Susan took a deep breath.

There was nothing wrong with a wish, right?

She wished to call her own the three little faces glowing with pride—pride at a cake they had frosted themselves, although Susan had been the one to make the iced flowers.

To claim Chelsea, at seven, already starting to take over some of Susan's sewing work on designing clothes for her multitude of Barbie dolls.

And Henry, at six already a gentleman. Or a knight. Or a superhero. Or just a boy with a cowlick that couldn't be tamed and hands that looked dirty bare seconds after a scrubbing.

And, of course, Baby Edward, who was two and a half and not really a baby anymore. But Henry and Chelsea kept raising the age limit on the word *baby,* like a reverse limbo bar. He'd be Baby Edward when he was fifteen.

Baby Edward stared at the cake and Susan knew exactly what he'd wish for.

Toys.

She reached out to touch his soft cheek and her attention was caught by the wedding band on her left hand. All that she had left of her own family, it looked like—but wasn't—a symbol of marital status. Instead, it was a reminder of her mother, left to her when she was just a child.

The ring brought to her mind the final, most secret, most selfish, most impossible wish that skittered across her mind as a wild mosaic of images: a vision of white, of tulle, of roses and real wedding rings, and passionate kisses on a bed covered with silk. It was what her parents had had, and their parents before them. It was what Susan wanted for herself.

She shook her head at her own silliness in wishing for...him. Wishing for him to hers.

And so, Susan having grown up to be realistic, maybe even a little too pragmatic, decided to wish only this: that this private moment at one end of the Radcliffe dining room table would last just a little longer.

"What are you going to wish for?" Chelsea asked.

"She won't get it if she tells," Henry said knowingly.

"Toys?" Baby Edward asked.

Susan smiled and kissed him on his forehead, inhaling his sweet baby smell. She touched the macaroni necklace that she wore—Chelsea's present. Henry and Baby Edward had drawn pictures that she had already folded carefully into her wallet for safekeeping.

Stretching out her moment...

"I won't tell you what I wish for," Susan said. "But, Baby Edward, you'll always have toys."

She took a deep breath, holding it long enough for the kids to take theirs. And then she blew. And they blew. Very hard, but still the candles fluttered as delicately as the wings of doves.

The dining room was thrown into complete black for a brief moment until Henry switched on the chandelier to its blazing glory.

It was amazing how quickly you forgot that the dining room was the size of a basketball court, Susan thought as she looked around the Louis-the-Fifteenth-inspired room.

"You'll get your wish!" Chelsea exclaimed, clapping her hands. "You got all the candles. You'll definitely get your wish."

"I already have," Susan replied.

Baby Edward reached out to steal a taste of icing, but Susan firmly pushed his hand away.

"Now how about we let Baby Edward have the piece with the red icing flower?" she asked.

She had placed the three flowers on the cake with extreme care, knowing that the pieces must be cut with precision. Baby Edward liked red things—fire trucks, valentines and red icing flowers. Chelsea liked yellow—the sun, lemonade and the yellow flowers. And Henry liked purple, the color of royalty, and Susan carefully cut the cake so each child got their favorite colored flower.

The cake had turned out pretty good on such short notice. Their father, Dean Radcliffe, had said only this morning he was coming home for the small family party to celebrate Susan's birthday.

Chelsea had invited him as the children sat planning Susan's party at the breakfast table.

"I'll be here with a cake and a special present for the birthday girl," he had promised.

"In time for dinner?" Henry had challenged.

Susan had felt a red, hot blush sweep over her, but luckily Dean Radcliffe didn't choose this moment to actually notice her.

He merely smiled at Henry.

"In time for dinner," he repeated.

Susan had made hot dogs and chips—but had put a steak in the refrigerator to thaw in case he did live up to his promise. She also made him a baked potato and salad, fixed a martini extradry, and got out the Harry Connick, Jr. CDs he liked. For an hour, Connick's soft and sultry jazz and the smell of home cooking had filled the house.

Then, around six, she had admitted to herself that he might, just might, not come home early. If she were truly honest with herself, she would know it was a billion to one shot that he would even remember his nanny's birthday.

Much less return from work with the promised cake, present, and on time.

She had started baking the cake while the children ate their dinner—feeding them their hot dogs was a hard concession to reality. But she knew she felt the disappointment in his not coming more acutely than the children. They scarcely missed the successive nights he didn't come home until they were already in bed.

Dean Radcliffe shouldn't be expected to come home early for his nanny's birthday. Susan sat back in her chair and shook her head at her own naive and heartfelt anticipation.

She had even worn her best blouse to top her usual sturdy jeans. She had hand-washed the blouse and mended the wrist where the seam was frayed. She had sewn the blouse years earlier from a piece of fine gold brocade she had found on sale at a junk store. She had thought at the time the color would set off her pale blond hair nicely.

But now Susan didn't think even a gold blouse could make her hair look all that good. It was damp with sweat from the oven's heat, held back by a scrunchie and dotted with icing. Even the prized blouse had some speckles of purple, yellow and red food dye.

She didn't feel like eating. Pushing her plate away, she took a couple of dog biscuits from her jeans pocket.

"I didn't forget you, Wiley," she said, holding them out to the eighty-pound German shepherd, who had awakened at the telltale sound of Susan rubbing those treats together.

The children savored their cake for several

minutes—Baby Edward eating only the icing and Chelsea making a hash of the fluffy insides—and then Henry asked the question he asked every night.

"Are you going to tell the story of the Eastman bears?"

"Only if Chelsea gets her pj's on and all of you brush your teeth."

Instant and complete obedience.

In ten minutes, Henry found his favorite pillow and spread out across the bottom of his elder sister's bed. Chelsea, in her Barbie doll nightgown, pulled the covers up to her neck. Susan sat at the head of the bed, Baby Edward on her lap. Lit by the golden hall light, the bedroom seemed a gateway into a wonderful paradise.

A paradise littered with discarded towels, children's clothes, toys and well-worn shoes.

A paradise guarded by Wiley.

A paradise ruled by bears.

Several times, Susan looked up to see the children's collection of Eastman teddy bears aligned on the dresser top. And she continued the tale she had told the night before, which was really just a continuation of the story of the night before that.

In fact, the story she had created about the Eastman bears extended as far back as any of the Radcliffe children could remember—though, in fact, Susan had only started working for the family the year before. A year after their mother's death.

Baby Edward's head drooped to Susan's shoulder. Henry squirmed, rolled around and finally found the perfect position. Chelsea closed her eyes.

I wish this were mine, Susan thought, letting herself be selfish for just one final second. And then she realized that she had already gotten her wish. They were here.

Maybe Dean Radcliffe wasn't with them, but her crush on him was so excruciating that he'd just make her nervous.

No, in a life already beat down with reality's harshness, Susan had a way of seeing the perfection in her day.

"And then Sister Bear walked all the way to the magic castle," she continued, finding her place in the story.

Dean Radcliffe tossed his keys on the hallway console and leafed through the pile of envelopes. Junk mail, requests for money, invitations to flashy charitable events Nicole would have loved. Why couldn't people just send money to help out their favorite charity—instead of requiring a black-tie event in return?

He pushed the mail to one side and walked through the darkened living room, carrying a cake box and a dozen roses.

Nicole was still in this house, though she had been dead for almost two years. He wondered if her death was what fueled his insatiable desire for work—never wanting to face the moment in the day when there as nothing left…but to come home. He raked his fingers through his blue-black hair and strode through the marbled hallway.

He paused as he reached the dining room. The crystal chandelier cast a faint golden glow on the remnants of a party—paper plates, noisemakers, half-eaten pieces of cake.

He shuddered.

Late again.

He really hadn't wanted to be.

Susan seemed like a nice nanny—in fact, she was the only person who would stay.

So he should make an effort.

Had wanted to make an effort.

Had made an effort.

He had spent a good two or three minutes with his secretary, Mrs. Witherspoon, telling her he wanted a cake, a dozen roses and a present from the jewelers. And Mrs. Witherspoon, who had worked for him since he graduated college and had worked for his father before him since the Jurassic Age, had taken care of everything with her usual pursed-mouthed efficiency.

He put the cake box down at the head of the table and pulled the small blue velvet jewelry box from the inside pocket of his charcoal gray suit jacket. He opened the box and studied the simple, silver-linked bracelet with three charms—two were silhouettes with Henry and Edward engraved in bold, block letters and one silhouette had pigtails and was engraved with Chelsea's name.

Simple. Nice. Festive.

But nothing a young woman could get the wrong idea about. A decidedly perfect nanny gift. Mrs. Witherspoon had done an excellent job.

Too bad he had missed the little party, but surely Susan couldn't expect that he would leave the strategic planning meeting for the Eastman Toy Company takeover just for her birthday!

No woman could expect that of him, especially not a sensible nanny like Susan.

Chapter Two

"And then Brother Bear came up with a great idea," Susan said. "He thought if they took a kitchen towel and made it into a sail, they could get across the big sherbet lake...."

"Daddy's home," Henry whispered.

"Daddy's home?" Chelsea hissed.

"Daddy?" Baby Edward asked groggily, opening one eye and then closing it. He snuggled farther into Susan's warm, soft bosom.

Wiley looked up from his sleep, arching one eyebrow in an imitation of alertness.

Dean Radcliffe climbed up the last landing up to the children's wing and appeared at the doorway, a tall shadow backlit by the hall light.

"Oh, Daddy," Henry said, poised between happiness and uncertainty about his father's mood.

"You missed Susan's birthday," Chelsea said accusingly.

"Now, Chelsea," Susan warned.

As Dean stood in the doorway, all Susan's sensible thoughts about him being out of reach flew out the window.

She loved him—and could kick herself for loving him.

And he, she reminded herself sternly, barely noticed her. His mind, as always, was on his work.

His only concession to the lateness of the hour was that his burgundy silk tie was pulled a bare inch away from the white Oxford shirt collar. His suit was severely, but most expensively, cut. His eyelids were sooty but, though he had left the house at six that morning, his emerald eyes were as piercing and quick as if he had just awakened.

He raked his fingers through his hair in a gesture that Susan recognized as meaning his head ached.

It should—his days were long, his work was grueling and he came home every day to children who reminded him of the wife he lost. With their blond hair, their freckles, their blue eyes so much like the wife who had died so tragically, so prematurely.

Susan was sure he must have loved his wife very much and mourned her deeply.

"I'm sorry, Mr. Radcliffe," Susan said, easing off of Chelsea's bed while managing to hold Baby

Edward in a comfortable sleeping position. "Children, give your father a kiss good-night. Then to bed. Henry, pick up your pillow—"

"No, it's all right. I'm interrupting," Dean said, raising his hand. "But I do want to talk to you in the study when you've put the children to bed."

Chelsea and Henry fell back onto the comforter in a mixture of relief and disappointment.

"Goody gum drops, we get to finish the story," Henry said.

"Daddy, I really do want to give you a good-night kiss," Chelsea said.

But Dean Radcliffe was already halfway down the hall to his study, followed by the ponderously slow but very loyal Wiley.

Ten minutes later, she went downstairs to the study with a tray piled high with two hot dogs, chips and the salad she had made earlier in the evening.

The steak was burnt beyond recognition and the baked potato shriveled like a piece of wadded-up paper. The martini pitcher was already washed, dried and put away in the bar armoire. Besides, she didn't want to remind him of the promise he had made—and broken.

"Susan, please sit down," Dean said as she came into the room. He looked at her with the wary but gracious expectancy he no doubt gave to all business associates, secretaries and clerks. "How kind of you to bring me dinner. I could have made something for myself."

"Actually, I just made a little more of what I made the kids," Susan said, conceding nothing about her hopes and dreams and efforts. She put the tray down on the only corner of the desk not covered with papers, and sat on the edge of one of the leather wing chairs opposite him. "You didn't eat yet?"

"No, I guess I didn't," he said. "I was too busy working out the details on the Eastman Toy deal. There's a lot of money riding on it."

He reached for a hot dog.

"How is it you always guess correctly the nights I don't have a business dinner and the ones when I'm able to come home in time for dinner?"

"Just intuition, I guess," she said. She didn't add that appearing at nine o'clock was hardly coming home in time for dinner.

She slipped Wiley a dog biscuit from her jeans pocket.

"I'm sorry about your birthday," he said stiffly, clearly not very practiced in apologies.

"It's all right," Susan said, shrugging.

"I wanted to talk to you about the children," Dean continued, showing his relief that she was understanding, that she knew her place in the household. "Tell me about how they're doing."

Susan swallowed the dryness in her mouth. She wondered if she was turning red—she did that when she was nervous. It was always this way with him, being around him. He made her excited and anxious and delighted all at the same time.

It was a crush. Just a stupid crush.

A crush she had rationalized and dissected and fought against so long and finally surrendered to so that it was now just a part of her personality, like her soft spot for children, weakness for chocolate and love of Audrey Hepburn movies.

Having a crush meant that whenever he was near, she noticed everything about him. Whether he was tired, whether he was sad. If he needed a haircut, if he was happy about some business deal.

She even noticed that he didn't notice her.

So she could have her dry mouth, could shake with the jitters, could feel her excitement, her face could have a bright crimson blush—and she never had to worry that he would embarrass her by even suspecting that he was the object of her adoration.

All he wanted was an update on the kids. All she wanted was the chance to be near him.

"Baby Edward pointed to the picture of a brachiosaurus in a book this morning and he could sort of say the name of it," she reported. "And Chelsea won the second-grade calla tournament today. She's very proud of her—"

"What's calla?"

"It's a board game. Uses numbers and counting. The second graders have been playing it."

"Strategy?"

"Yes, it uses strategy. Sort of like checkers."

"Good. Chelsea's got a good head for scoping out the competition."

Actually, Susan just thought Chelsea was a bright, sweet little girl who had played a lot of calla games with her friends.

"Henry's teacher told me when I picked him up that he's doing much better with sounding out blends. And he got invited to Michael's house for a play date this afternoon."

"Excellent. He must begin making those vital connections."

"You mean friendships?"

"Yes, of course, friendships."

As Susan continued the update of domestic events, she was amazed again at how, even as busy, as distant as he was, Dean Radcliffe knew every detail of his children's life. He puzzled over Henry's phonics problems, asked about whether Chelsea's best friend, Martina, had recovered from chicken pox and reminded Susan that all three were due for their six-month dental visit.

On the other hand, maybe he was the kind of businessman who remembered the birthdays of his clients' secretaries and sent gifts to trusted employees at Christmas.

He certainly was that way with the children.

"Susan, I'll have my secretary get Edward a T-shirt with a brachiosaurus," Dean said. "Sort of a congratulations-on-learning-your-dinosaurs gift."

Susan nodded, although she didn't like it when Dean counted on Mrs. Witherspoon to pick up things for the children. Maybe Dean should consider telling Baby Edward himself that he was proud—but it wasn't her place to make suggestions.

"Will that be all?" she asked.

"No, one more thing," Dean said, finishing up his hot dog. "I want that storytelling to stop."

Susan flushed. She had thought that might be coming. They had had this conversation before. She gulped, hating to have done something contrary.

"I'm sorry. It's just the kids were acting up tonight, didn't want to go to bed," she rationalized. "And they seem to like the story so much."

"I don't want their heads filled with fantasy," Dean said, his voice suddenly icily determined. Susan shivered under the personal power this man had—if he treated his business adversaries this way then he certainly deserved his reputation for always getting his way—without ever having to raise his voice.

"I'm sorry, Mr. Radcliffe."

"They need to face reality. Not be distracted by fiction," he added. "Besides, the Eastman Bear Company is ripe for my purchase precisely because of the muddled thinking promoted by such dreaming."

"But the children like it—hearing stories about the bears."

"I would suggest you reading to them about history or science or animals," he replied curtly in a way that left no doubt this was no mere suggestion, it was an order.

Susan bit back a retort.

He was so close, so close to connecting to these children, Susan thought. But then he couldn't do it. He wanted to love them, did love them, but couldn't get close enough to them to see that they were wonderful children and having a few moments of whimsy at the end of the day wouldn't turn them into wimps or daydreamers. He was so close to being a real father to them, but he couldn't do it. She knew the death of his wife had hurt him greatly. She wondered what kind of man he had been before the tragedy.

Because she loved him, she could forgive him the kind of man he was now.

And wish that someday he would change.

She stood up.

"It won't happen again," she said.

"Good. Oh, Susan, I nearly forgot," he said, pulling a velvet box from under a pile of papers. "Your birthday."

She approached the desk, swallowing back a sad-

ness mingled with anticipation. She wished she
hadn't wanted his present, wished she didn't care.
She only knew she did. She approached the desk
and he smiled—the same charming smile that had
gotten him everything in life.

"Thank you," she said.

"You're welcome," he answered and turned his
attention to some paperwork in front of him. "And
happy birthday. By the way, what's that perfume
you're wearing? It's very beautiful."

He asked the question as if he were asking what
time the trains ran, but still he asked it. Her breath
caught. She looked into his emerald eyes as he
waited for her answer. And for a moment, a scant
moment, her heart soared as she knew he had noticed her, really noticed her.

She felt a rising heat in her body, confusing as
it was enticing.

How could he do it? With just a look, just a word
he could make her quiver.

She was nuts—he didn't give her a thought other
than in her capacity as nanny.

And yet he had just noticed her, had noticed her
scent.

He noticed her as a woman.

Her heart soared and then fell flat with a *thad-
dump!* as her body heat made her scent blossom
and even she could recognize its source.

"Cake," she said blandly. "I smell like cake."

Chapter Three

"That was real close," Chelsea said in a small voice.

"Real close," Henry blubbered.

"Just pay attention to the story," Susan urged. "Then you won't notice the thunder. Now where was I? Oh, yes, the Continental Congress appointed five men to write a letter to the King explaining why the colonies should not be taxed under the Parliamentary—"

"Can you tell us about Eastman Bears again?" Chelsea asked.

"Sorry, honey, it's not…not a good idea," Susan said, thinking of their father's new restrictions on what they should read. "Besides, I told you the whole story."

"No, you didn't," Henry pointed out.

"Bears," Baby Edward begged. He didn't like the blue book about the American Revolution. Not even the pictures of Benjamin Franklin, the Liberty Bell or the midnight ride of Paul Revere.

The nightstand lamp flickered on and off. Susan glanced only briefly at the window, determined to not let the children see that she was worried. The wind was fast and furious—the massive Radcliffe oaks creaked and groaned as their branches were yanked back and forth. Hail and rain slapped against the windowpanes and the sky was a sickly yellow and black. No wonder they called this part of northern Illinois "Tornado Alley."

"I wish Daddy was home," Henry said dismally.

"Me, too," said Chelsea.

"Me, thweeeeh," Baby Edward added.

Clap!

Chelsea and Henry leapt into Susan's arms at the crack of blazing light and thunder. Susan hugged all three children and watched the lamp flutter and die, plunging the bedroom into darkness.

The book on the American Revolution slid from her lap to the floor.

"I want my daddy!" Chelsea cried in great, convulsive gulps. "I'm scared!"

Baby Edward howled.

"All right, all right," Susan soothed. "Now let's try to be a little braver."

"I can't," Chelsea exclaimed.

"I can't, either," Henry said.

Susan looked around the room, blinking to adjust to the darkness. Familiar furniture seemed like ominous prowling monsters and the curtains looked like unearthly ghosts.

And the candles were safely tucked in the dining room hutch, waiting for dinner parties that hadn't been given since the mistress of the house had died.

She disengaged herself from the children enough to shove her hand into Chelsea's toy box. Rooting around, she pulled out the Teenage Mutant Ninja Turtle flashlight. She flicked it on, shooting out a small but comforting speck of light.

"Calm down, all three of you. The Bear family survived a storm much worse than this without a single tear."

Henry was the first to catch on. He gulped down his sobs and wiped his runny nose with his sleeve.

"They did? Not a single tear?"

"It was a much bigger storm than this one," Susan said, guilty that she was going against her employer's wishes but certain he would understand. Just this once.

She hustled them back into the safe bed, opening her arms wide enough to encompass them all. Even Henry, who sometimes considered himself too old for her embraces.

She started another tale, a story she made up as

she went along, cuing her words to the reactions of her charges. She had described the storm, the bears, their bravery and was winding things up, when they heard the first anguished yelps.

"It's Wiley!" Henry shrieked.

"Oh, no!" Susan cried.

The children leapt from the bed to the window, Susan behind them. Illuminated by the lightning, the pitiful, wet, sobbing Wiley stood in the courtyard—pulling at the chain that tied him to the steel shed out in back of the Radcliffe oak trees.

"The landscape service must have forgotten to let him loose after they mowed the lawn," Susan said.

"Bring him back in!" Chelsea demanded.

"Yeah, get him!" Henry begged.

Susan stared in horror at the poor dog and then at her charges. If she did nothing, Wiley's pain and terror would be unbearable—for all of them.

But if she went downstairs and left the three children on their own...

"I'll go down there, but you have to stand right here," she said. "And don't move. And take care of Baby Edward. Chelsea, you're in charge."

She left them the flashlight and some comforting kisses. In the hall, she felt her way, hand over hand, along the walls of the night-shrouded house. Down the steps, through the cavernous pitch-black dining room. At last she reached the kitchen. She flung open the back door, then fell back as the wind slammed it right back against her. She landed hard.

She scrambled up, grabbed the door handle and shoved with all her might. A sudden vacuum created by the unruly wind sucked the door outward, and she lurched onto the back porch. Downed branches and ripped leaves, slathered to the porch with rain, made it slippery going.

Out past the courtyard, Wiley moaned for her, his eyes pleading for relief.

Woman and dog jumped as the sky cracked in two with a bang and a burst of light.

That was close, Susan thought. Must have hit right near the orchard behind the formal Radcliffe gardens. Swallowing the tight lump of fear, she charged down the steps and across the courtyard.

She looked back once through the sheets of rain to see three ghostly faces pressed against the window of the second-floor back bedroom. Then she reached for Wilcy and he lapped her hand as she fumbled with the chain at his neck.

"It's all right, Wiley, you're safe now," Susan comforted. She found the grip, and released him. He raced for the back door, slipping once but recovering as if the very hounds of hell were chasing him.

Susan felt a gentle tap on her shoulder and, still holding the metal chain, she turned around. She looked down at the bracelet Dean Radcliffe had given her—its little charms twinkling in the eerie storm light. She hadn't wanted to wear it, hadn't wanted to admit it meant something to her to receive a gift from him. But she wore it now—always, long after they grew up, the children would be in her memories. She hoped she would get over Dean.

A quivering light burst from the shed and slithered up the chain to the twinkling bracelet. She felt fire squeezing her wrists. And then came the roar of thunder, close against her ear.

"Daddy, you gotta come home." Henry gulped, then choked on a sob. "Daddy, it's just like the night Mommy...."

Dean Radcliffe picked up the receiver on the speaker phone and with a single silencing glance at the executives around the conference table, leaned back in his chair.

"What's just like—" He hesitated and took a deep breath. "What's just like that night?"

"The lightning!" Henry cried.

Dean glanced out his sixty-fourth-floor office window to the black sky. Clouds hung low, so low it seemed he could grab their swollen mounds. There was a crack of lightning in the distance.

It all came back to him—even now the memory was as sickening as it had been two years ago.

Nicole's body, her car at the bottom of the ravine

where the Radcliffe property line met the street, the car radio still playing the heavy-metal music she loved so much, her blond hair thrown forward across her still, frozen face.

"Henry, get Susan on the phone," he ordered his son, more curtly perhaps as he struggled to squelch his own emotions.

"That's the problem," Henry said. "Susan's outside."

Unbidden, the scent of sugar and vanilla came to him. He batted it away with a surge of anger. She was clearly negligent, leaving the frightened children to fend for themselves. He'd have to talk to her.

"What's she doing outside?"

He stood up, his tall frame making the office look as if it had been furnished with treasures from a dollhouse. He raked a callused hand through his hair. Savvy executives knew he was fighting off a headache—they had seen that gesture many times during tense negotiations. And nothing in recent years had been more tension filled than the attempted purchase of the Eastman Bear Company.

Indistinct sobs crackled from the speaker phone.

"Henry!" Dean yelled.

Someone else came on the line.

"Daddy, it's Chelsea. Please come home."

"If Susan's outside, get me..." He thought for a minute, and then remembered the terrible truth.

There wasn't a housekeeper who would stay in the isolated and gloomy Radcliffe house. There wasn't a maid who had lasted longer than a day. And he had fired the groundskeeper two days after Nicole's death; as he remembered that man, his jaws clenched in suppressed rage.

The problem was there was no one to care for his children except Susan.

Dependable, responsible, nearly invisible Susan. If she wasn't there...

"There's no one here, Daddy," Chelsea said quietly. "Susan went outside to save Wiley."

Dean scribbled a note to Mrs. Whitherspoon and passed it across the table to her. "Call 911, send them to the house," it said.

"Are you hurt?" he demanded.

"No," Chelsea said in a very small voice.

"Are Henry and Edward all right?"

"Yes, but we're very scared."

Dean took a deep breath, and his emerald eyes skittered across the conference room at the two dozen executives who had been working through profit-loss statements, annual reports, spreadsheets and payroll estimations for the purchase of the Eastman Bear Company.

"Daddy, it's just like Mommy," Chelsea said.

He closed his eyes, wishing very much that she wouldn't say that. He had worked so hard to get on with his life.

"You're just saying that because it's a storm, just like on…that night."

"No, Daddy," Chelsea said. "I'm saying that because…because she's dead."

Dean dropped the phone and leapt across the table, making the receptionist's desk in the lobby in four seconds.

"Fire department will be out there in ten minutes," Mrs. Witherspoon cried out to his shadow.

"Not soon enough," he muttered.

He punched the elevator button with his fist, then decided to take the stairs. He hit the parking lot in less than a minute, leapt into his midnight-colored Porsche and skidded out onto the street.

Chelsea was so right, he thought, as he sped down the rain-soaked streets of Chicago. It was just like that long-ago night of violent tempers and recriminations. He remembered driving home, angered at… Well, those memories were too painful to go over.

He reached the house before the fire trucks—although, to their credit, he could hear the sirens from a distance.

He screeched to a halt at the point where the circular drive met the front colonnade. His three children cowered just inside the door.

"Are you all right?" he demanded, taking the

steps three at a time and yanking open the beveled glass door.

"We're all right." Chelsea gulped. "It's...it's Susan."

Though he wanted to pick up a howling Edward, to smooth Henry's trembling lip, to brush away Chelsea's tears, he knew he'd better go first to the body of his children's nanny.

Besides, for the past two years, he had found himself totally unable to handle any of his children's emotions.

"Now this, now this," he muttered as he swept through the entrance hall, the living room, the library and out onto the breakfast room porch. Rain lashed against the French doors, and gurgling waters from overflowing gutters swept through the cobblestone courtyard.

He opened the back door and then he saw her. The inert body. Susan? He tried to remember any detail of the woman who had cared for his children for the past year.

But to him, she was the only nanny who had lasted, and there had been fourteen others who had left before her—some lasting no more than a day. He was hard on people, he knew that, and regret welled up in him as he realized that if he were only easier to work for, he might have had a full-time housekeeper, or maid—someone else besides the woman who came twice-a-week—to bring the dog in.

He took the steps two at a time and crouched down at her rain-soaked body.

He opened the palm of her hand, and nearly broke down in uncharacteristic tears as he saw she still held the metal clasp of Wiley's chain.

He looked heavenward, wondering at a world in which there could be such random and senseless horror.

She had given her life for his children's dog.

He rolled her over carefully, put his hand underneath her head and pulled her up into his arms.

Gently, so very gently. She deserved the deepest respect in death even if she had never, to his knowledge, had much respect accorded to her in life.

Hadn't the agency said something about her not having had much of a family?

Well, maybe that's the only thing that would make a nanny willing to put up with him.

He looked at the closed eyes, the pale skin with drops of rain like dewdrops on rose petals. He touched the budlike lips. He stroked away the wet, thick tendrils of golden hair. He knew it wasn't right, but his eyes drifted to the swell of her breasts revealed by the rain-drenched T-shirt. She had been beautiful, in her own fresh and innocent kind of way.

He had never noticed. Never noticed at all.

He thought of the life that had been taken away from her, of all the opportunities that a sweet, gentle girl like her had lost. The future—the possibility of finding someone, of having children, of having a life.

All for Wiley, a twelve-year-old German shepherd.

All because of his own stupidity and hard-heartedness—there should have been someone else here to worry about the dog, someone else to help out around the house.

Hadn't she just had a birthday? He searched his memory and realized that he hadn't even been able to offer her a day off. Hadn't even managed to get home in time for a shared dinner. Had delegated the purchase of her birthday present to Mrs. Witherspoon. He noticed the twinkling of the three-charm bracelet.

He shook his head sadly.

And then, suddenly, her darkly lashed eyes fluttered open. She looked up at him, smiled at first tentatively and then joyously. Those amber eyes he had never noticed before now seemed to him to be the most beautiful jewels he had ever seen.

Simply because she was alive.

She squeezed her arms around his neck and his first thought was that he would never, ever embarrass her by reminding her that she had acted most unnannylike by hugging him.

It was a shock—to both of them—and perfectly forgivable, Dean reminded himself.

Many people acted foolishly in the face of death.

"Darling," she said. "Darling, I'm so glad you're home."

And she put her mouth on him and kissed him, really kissed him, while hail the size of Ping-Pong balls pelted the yard and the fire truck came to a screeching halt at the front steps of the Radcliffe mansion.

Chapter Four

Three hours later, after a conference call made from the hospital lobby to reschedule the day's meeting with the owner of Eastman Toys, Dean Radcliffe swept up the hospital staircase with an oversize bouquet of dazzlingly white and pink tea roses that had been dropped off by Mrs. Witherspoon.

He stopped at the fourth-floor's nurses' station.

"Susan...uh," he said, snapping the fingers of his free hand as he struggled to remember the last name of his nanny. "Susan. She was brought in this evening. The emergency room nurse said she'd been transferred up here from the emergency room. It was a lightning accident. She was struck by lightning. Susan...uh...Susan...uh..."

Susan something or other.

He couldn't remember her last name.

Had he ever known what it was?

When he had called the office, Mrs. Witherspoon hadn't even known. And Mrs. Witherspoon knew everything, with the cool, unruffled efficiency of a computer.

He had told Mrs. Witherspoon to find someone, anyone from the agency who could take over this crisis. He ordered her to make arrangements to pay for Susan's hospitalization and recovery. And a generous severance pay to help her if she didn't want to return to work.

He hoped she'd want to come back.

The alternative would be a disaster because the agency had warned him many times that it was difficult to find anyone who would work for him at the Radcliffe Estate.

He shoved down the sensation that had haunted him for the past hours, a memory he had dodged by concentrating on the changing profit-loss ratios of Eastman Bears and stock option prices.

Still, the memory nagged at him.

She had kissed him.

She had grabbed him by the collar and kissed him in a way that was most un-Susan-like.

In a way that made him think of stars and fire-crackers and roller-coaster rides and trips to the beach. In a way that lingered on his lips like a caress, even now he could remember the feel. And when he had been most thoroughly kissed by her, she had pulled away and looked up at him with frank sensuality and the breezy confidence of a woman his equal. Straight into his eyes without a whisper of the deference he had unconsciously come to expect from the women in his life.

Not like the Susan he knew at all!

As the paramedics poured out onto the courtyard, he had picked her up, shielding her face with his jacket—but it hadn't been the rain he had feared, it was the notion of strangers seeing her so...so naked and open and womanly and sensual.

When she was brought back to her right senses, she would be appalled.

She had obviously been very traumatized. Would never remember it and be very embarrassed if she were told about it.

Which he didn't intend on doing.

He found himself staring into the eyes of the fourth-floor station nurse. And remembering Susan's beautiful amber eyes, eyes that he had never before noticed.

"Susan," he repeated more slowly, wondering if the feel of her name on his lips would ever be the same. The name didn't sound quite so efficient and no-nonsense. The name Susan conjured up images of such intensity that he closed his eyes and counted to ten in an effort to get a grip on himself.

"Your wife, Mr. Radcliffe?" the nurse, a big blonde with a horsey jaw, supplied. "She's resting comfortably. In room 403. Here, there's some paperwork in her file. You're supposed to sign two releases for the Cat scan we performed and..."

Dean opened his eyes to an inch-thick sheaf of forms the nurse had flapped down on the counter.

"No, no, no," he said, the roses trembling in his arms. "She's not my wife."

"Not your wife?" the nurse questioned, frowning.

"Not my wife," Dean confirmed, again reviewing his nanny's very odd behavior. She had called him darling. She had kissed him. He touched his lips, where he thought he might still feel her kiss.

She must have been in some sort of shock.

Poor, poor Susan.

Now he was the one having problems.

An older man in a white jacket approached the nurses' station. He leaned close to Dean.

"But, Mr. Radcliffe, your wife is in room 403. Recovering nicely," he said. "The Cat scan indicated some problem areas, but considering the shock she took, we're all quite amazed that she's doing as well as she is."

"She's my children's nanny," Dean said brusquely, determinedly putting the memory of her kiss aside. "My wife...my wife...my wife is—was actually was a woman named Nicole and she's..."

"Relax. You look entirely too agitated," the man soothed. "Please, let me introduce myself. I'm Dr. Sugar. Sam Sugar. I treated your wife this evening in the ER. When she came in, her blood pressure was 80 over 40 and her heartbeat was erratic but essentially strong and we started with a potassium drip—"

"The woman who was brought in this evening is not my wife," Dean interrupted.

"But it says right here that she's your wife," the nurse said, holding up the chart.

Her square-jawed stare made clear that as far as she was concerned, that ended the matter. Hospital forms were never wrong.

"She's not my wife. Maybe there's been some confusion," Dean said. "She's actually my children's nanny. If she told you she's my wife she's very much mistaken."

"Admitting on the first floor says she's your wife," the nurse insisted.

"Maybe it's Braxton-Myers shock," Dr. Sugar mused.

"What's that?"

"Disturbance on the left lower ventricle of the brain," Dr. Sugar explained. "People who have been struck by lightning often have very strange neurological responses."

"Lightning made her think she's my wife?"

"Most Braxton-Myers experiences are short-term," Dr. Sugar reassured.

"How short-term?"

Dr. Sugar shrugged.

"Hours, days, weeks, sometimes a few months."

"You don't know when she's going to stop thinking she's my wife?"

"She's very beautiful." Dr. Sugar shrugged. "Wouldn't be the worst thing to happen to a man."

"I've never noticed whether any employee is beautiful or not," Dean said coldly. "Least of all, the woman I hire to provide child care."

But he had noticed—if only this evening. In the rain, her hair slicked back with rain, her face flushed like a tea rose and her eyes a clear, brilliant golden shade.

"A man would have to be blind not to give her a look," Dr. Sugar said slyly. "And you don't look very blind."

"I make it a practice never to notice the physical attributes of my employees."

He saw the exchange of knowing looks between doctor and nurse. He could almost hear the disbelieving "uh-huh" that passed silently between them.

"I'll just put those roses in a vase," the nurse said, efficiently sweeping the flowers out of his arms. "For your wife."

"She's not my wife..." Dean protested, his

voice trailing to nothing as he realized the nurse was halfway down the hall with the roses waving gaily over her shoulder.

"Susan was registered at the emergency room under the name Radcliffe," Dr. Sugar pointed out. "And you yourself carried her from the ambulance into the emergency room. I heard you were quite distraught. Wouldn't let anyone else touch her."

"I was acting like a concerned employer."

"She's asked for the children, by name, several times."

"She's a devoted nanny."

"And she has a bracelet that you gave her with the children's silhouettes as charms, has a wedding ring..."

"I didn't give her that."

Dr. Sugar looked at him archly.

"I did give her the bracelet," Dean conceded. "Actually, my secretary picked it out. But I didn't give her the wedding ring. You don't believe me, do you?"

"I don't want to guess at the relationship between you and Mrs. Radcliffe—I mean, Susan."

"There isn't any!"

The two men were silent.

"All right." Dr. Sugar sighed. "But please understand, we now have a little problem. A medical problem. I've got a patient in there who is only now stabilizing, whose blood pressure is back up, whose heart beat is increasingly regular and who is something of a medical miracle because she's able to breathe without the help of a respirator."

"So she's better."

"Yes she is, and I'd appreciate it if you don't screw it up," Sugar said, jabbing Dean's shoulder with his index finger.

"What's that supposed to mean?" Dean demanded, thinking that if the doctor were twenty years younger his jab wouldn't go unchallenged.

"I'll schedule tests for Braxton-Myers disturbance tomorrow, but buddy, for tonight you're her husband whether you want to be or not."

"What!"

"I don't want her to suffer another shock tonight by having you charge in there telling her she's the nanny—I want you to go in there right now and play along with her. Play a nice husband, keep her calm and relaxed. We'll sort everything out later, when she's stronger."

Dean was outraged.

"Why don't I just go home and she can go to sleep tonight secure in her belief that she's Mrs. Radcliffe?"

"Because she's been asking for you. She's really very devoted to you. Perfectly wonderful. I mean, if she were a wife. Don't worry, Mr. Radcliffe, I'll get those tests scheduled for the morning."

Dean ran his fingers through his hair and resolved that he personally would call the nanny's employment agency.

Susan's family, her real family, must be found.

Susan Radcliffe looked at the drawings Henry and Baby Edward had made for her birthday. How glad she was that she had her wallet so she could have their pictures with her. Her head hurt so much from the accident that it was hard to conjure up their images in her mind—and she so missed them. She hoped they hadn't been too frightened by the accident.

She also told herself she'd better get to the Secretary of State's office tomorrow morning to get the name on her driver's licence switched to Radcliffe. Having her maiden name on all her I.D. had thrown admitting for a loop. It had taken her over an hour to convince them she was Dean's wife—for the life of her, she couldn't think why she hadn't had her I.D. changed long ago....

Putting that niggling thought out of her mind, she returned her attention to the children. She wanted to talk to them, to comfort them, to hold them— oh, when would she get to go home?

"Dean?" she asked softly as the door opened.

Her husband hesitated.

"Darling, come on in. It's all right. I'm really much better." She patted the bed. "Sit down right next to me. How are the children?"

He opened his mouth. Shut it again. Then opened it again.

"They're with Mrs. Witherspoon," he said finally. "She's teaching them how to send faxes to our European and Asian branch offices."

Susan made a little face.

"She's a sweet woman, but I don't think she knows much about kids. Still, I'm grateful to her for taking care of them," she added. She scrutinized Dean. "Darling, why are you standing there like that? I'm not contagious, you know."

He swallowed hard and warily positioned himself two inches closer, by the television affixed to the wall.

Susan crimsoned.

"You're angry at me. And maybe you have every right to be. I should have brought Wiley in earlier when the lawn guys left. I forgot and got so caught up with the kids that I just wasn't thinking."

She closed her eyes and tears splashed against her cheeks.

"Are you all right?"

"No, I'm not all right," she sputtered.

Dean rushed to her side, putting his arms around her.

She felt his tentativeness. It wasn't like him. He was ordinarily a powerful, confident lover whose embraces were strong and virile.... Her head throbbed with a sudden stabbing pain as she tried to remember the details of his style of lovemaking.

Giving up, she simply looked up into his eyes, clear emerald eyes that had never, not once, failed to give her strength and calmness.

He looked away.

"It's not your fault," he said, staring with great interest at the window. "And I'm not angry at all. In fact, I'm very grateful that you saved Wiley's life. You nearly gave your life to save my children's dog."

She looked heavenward.

"Dean, they're not 'my' children, they're 'our' children. And it's not gratitude between us. It's love."

He flinched at the *L* word and she reminded herself that sometimes Dean had trouble with emotions. He felt the entire spectrum of emotions as well as anyone else, but he just didn't like to talk about them. She had learned to live with that, had learned to read his heart as easily as a newspaper. And knew enough to make her emotional needs known in bluntly physical terms.

"Just kiss me, darling," she said, knowing that he would have no trouble expressing himself. No trouble sharing his confidence, no trouble kissing away her fears.

He leaned forward and very solemnly, very softly brushed his lips against her forehead.

And then leaned back, his face rigid, jaws clenched.

This really was the limit!

"Dean, what has gotten into you?" Susan demanded, her voice rising with irritation. "I already apologized for having left Wiley out and putting him in danger. I didn't even put up a fuss when you got on the cellular phone two minutes after we got to the emergency room. Tomorrow I'm going to be perfectly fine and be able to go home so I won't interfere with whatever's going on at the office. I don't understand how you can hold back from me just because you're..."

She saw a funny little wiggling in the corner of her right eye, a herringbone tear on her vision. The doctor had warned her that this visual disturbance might occur if she got overexcited.

A neurological problem, he said. It would come just before the pain, pain that would require medication. She didn't want that—didn't want any medication to make her drowsy and disoriented.

She was confused enough already.

But not so confused that she didn't remember that she wanted everything to go smoothly so she could get back home tomorrow morning.

And having to beg for medication would only push her release back another day.

She pushed her fingers up against her temples and made it better. At least, a little bit better.

"Susan, I mean, darling, please don't get upset," Dean begged urgently. "Here, I'll kiss you. I promise. Will it make you feel better if I do?"

"Don't do me any favors," Susan growled, keeping her fingers pressed very tightly against her face.

"I'm not doing you a favor. I want to kiss you. I really want to. I just want to make sure that no matter what, even if you feel…differently in a few days, that you won't blame me for having done it."

Susan stared out from behind the lattice pattern of her fingers.

"Who in their right mind would blame you for kissing your wife? Especially if she asked?"

Oooh, he really was making her head hurt!

"Right mind, that's exactly what I'm talking about," Dean countered. "In their right mind. When you're in your right mind would you want me to kiss you?"

"Are you accusing me of being crazy?"

"Absolutely not. Darling, I mean, Susan, promise me that you understand that I'm only kissing you because you asked.…" He paused when she took her fingers away from her temples long enough to give him a murderous look. "I'm only kissing you because…because…well, just because.…"

Dean gave up talking, which was good because

when he wasn't talking business, he wasn't very good at it at all.

Instead, he did what he was better at, what he was the very best at. He pulled her hands away from her head and put them down on the bed, covering them with his own. And then he leaned forward, offering her his own familiar scent, a mixture of citrus and musk.

And then her husband finally kissed her.

At first he held back. Held everything back. He offered her the lightest touch of his lips, dry and closed. She nearly shoved him away and ordered him from the room. He was acting so darned prissy!

But she had been made for him, her body molded to his sexual needs since the day they were married…how many years ago? Her head kind of hurt when she thought about it, so she stopped thinking about it.

She let her body do what it did naturally. She came to him, wiggling her body down on the sheets so that she was at just the right angle for more. She enticed him, seduced him, surrendered to him, pleasured him—and in doing so, pleasured herself.

Her lips parted, taking in his tongue. She leaned her head backward so that his flesh could come into her mouth more fully. Deeply, passionately, his tongue demanded and won responses that surprised her with their intensity.

Heavens! She was a married woman, had been married...how many years?

No, no, don't think about it now.

Especially not now when it was so wonderful. Made the headache disappear completely.

Funny, her response to him must be heightened by the accident, she reasoned. Because his kiss had the ardor of early courtship and her response had all the power of awakening love....

He put one strong arm around her, splaying his fingers on the small of her back. Her nipples ached as they rubbed against the stern fabric of his suit. She moaned throatily—he had always welcomed, even encouraged, love sounds.

And since he had been her first, and only, lover, she naturally did what he liked. What they both liked.

Abruptly he released her, as the nurse—who had entered unnoticed—slapped a vase of white long-stem roses on the nightstand.

"Some nanny!" the nurse harrumphed before stalking out the door.

"What did she mean by that?" Susan asked.

"I have no idea," Dean muttered.

She admired the flowers, thanked Dean for them and then noticed he seemed dazed.

"Are you all right?" she asked. "Remember, darling, I'm the one who's been struck by lightning."

He shook his head.

"I'm not all right," he said miserably. "Su-san...Susan, no matter what happens in the next few days, no matter how you feel about me, no matter whether you decide to come back or not, I just want you to know you're...you're...won-derful."

She flung her arms around him, hugging him tightly to her. She ignored every confusing thing he had presented to her. His mind must be befuddled by the accident, she rationalized.

But she didn't have to rationalize how happy she was to be in her husband's arms.

"Darling, I know how hard it is for you to talk about feelings," she said. "And I want you to know that's the most romantic thing you've ever said to me since...well, since whenever we got married."

Chapter Five

Dean stared at Dr. Sugar in disbelief.

"Nothing?" he asked.

"Absolutely nothing," Dr. Sugar confirmed. "There is no physical evidence of neurological disturbance."

"And that means?"

"That means we have no surgery, no lasers, no magic pills that can change her mind about you."

"So what do I do?"

"It would appear that if she takes it easy for a few weeks, we'll see a complete recovery," Dr. Sugar replied, sidestepping Dean's unspoken question about how to persuade Susan that she wasn't his wife. "Susan can go home today and be up and running at full speed in a month. She's a living miracle."

"That's great news," Dean said, wondering how he'd tell Susan she wasn't his wife.

He sipped at the harsh coffee dispensed from the machine in the doctor's conference room. Piled on the table were the charts, scans, X rays and test results Sugar had reviewed with him.

Dean liked to have all the answers, and Dr. Sugar had certainly given him answers.

But Susan's kisses had left a lot of questions lingering in his head. Uncomfortable questions about how he could be so easily caught off guard by a woman's touch.

A woman who had been a mere shadow in his life days ago—as real to him as any of the other things that made his life run so efficiently.

A toaster for breakfast.

A fax machine for transmission of documents.

The telephone conferencing system for keeping in touch with business associates.

And his nanny to take care of his children.

"Your wife is a very lucky woman," Sugar mused. "Most people—even a healthy young woman like Susan—wouldn't survive this kind of shock."

"She's not my wife," Dean reminded the doctor. "If there's nothing in her Cat scan, nothing in her blood test, why does she think she's my wife?"

Sugar shrugged, as if this question of matrimonial identity weren't nearly as important as Dean considered it.

"When I say nothing is wrong with her, that just means we can't find something measurable, something we can point to on an X ray. Sometimes, patients who survive lightning strikes develop all kinds of powers and intuitions. And sometimes delusions—this one seems pretty harmless. She's not claiming to be the president."

"It's harmless only if you're not her husband!"

"If you want to go in and tell her now that she's not your wife," Sugar said, choosing his words with care, "then I have no objection. But please try to be sensitive to her condition. She could have a relapse at any time and I'm sure you don't want that on your conscience."

"No, I don't," Dean conceded, remembering the terror he had felt when he had thought she was dead, when he was sure it was his fault.

"Besides, she'll figure it out soon enough, I'm sure," Sugar continued. "Her memories will eventually bubble up to the surface and she'll figure out exactly who she is. But I don't have any pill or treatment that will make it happen any sooner."

Shaking his head in frustration, Dean stood up and held out his hand to the doctor.

"My secretary, Mrs. Witherspoon, will be in touch to pay for Susan's stay," he said.

Sugar held on to his hand long enough to catch Dean's attention.

"If I were twenty years younger," the doctor said. "I'd simply smile and say 'Yes, dear' when a woman as pretty as Susan said she was my wife. A man couldn't do much better than to call her his own."

"I suppose so," Dean agreed dryly, shoving aside memories of the touch of her lips. "You're right. She'll make a good wife. To somebody else."

He said goodbye to Dr. Sugar, picked up Susan's worn canvas suitcase in which he had shoved her meager belongings and walked down the corridor to room 403.

He'd have a talk with Susan. After she understood she wasn't his wife, he'd check her out of the hospital and have a taxi take her to the rehab center Mrs. Witherspoon had contacted.

Hopefully, Susan wouldn't be so embarrassed by her delusion that she'd do something crazy like cry, but he had to allow for that possibility.

By the time he reached the end of the hallway, Dean had calculated that if he allowed ten or fifteen minutes for being as "sensitive" as Dr. Sugar suggested, he'd still be out of this hospital in less than half an hour. Because he was sure that Susan—sensible, hardworking Susan—would be so mortified that she'd want him to leave.

In fact, the most sensitive thing to do would be to leave right away!

Then he'd get back to the office, grateful that the time he had taken off could be made up. A few late nights this week and he'd be back up to speed on the takeover bid for Eastman Bear Company. He wondered briefly at how he had packed his days so tightly that a few hours away from the office had driven his company dangerously close to disaster.

He paused at the doorway, caught up in a fantasy that skittered across his thoughts as lightly as a wind-tossed leaf. What if he had a wife like Susan? Hell, what if she were his, really his?

Susan, softly beautiful Susan.

Beautiful? Well, he guessed, she could be beautiful.

Hadn't really noticed before.

But Sugar was right—a man couldn't do better. Kind, sensitive, good with his children—and sexy in an innocent, fresh kind of way.

The kind of woman who made a man want to make love—after he'd put a ring on her finger.

Ridiculous! He shoved the door open and went in, prepared to confront this delusional nanny as efficiently as he dealt with any other problem employee.

But the woman on the bed didn't look like an ordinary employee, didn't look like the Susan he remembered. Her hair was sleekly combed to a fiery golden color. Her eyes were bright and dazzlingly amber. Her smiling face was set off with a cheery cranberry-colored lipstick.

And somehow she made a hospital gown look downright sexy!

"Darling, hello. We have a visitor!" Susan exclaimed.

She held out her arms for an embrace, which he hesitated to accept—and then he looked up into the face of a man who bore an uncanny resemblance to a slug.

Which this man was. A slug.

Rather than embarrass Susan by declining her outstretched arms, he gave her a quick, hopefully ambiguous-looking embrace and glowered at the man slouched in the chair beside the bed.

He didn't want the slug getting any ideas.

"Burt Warber." Dean grimaced in a barely civil acknowledgment. "What are you doing here?"

Warber shoved his glasses back up his nose and blubbered an unintelligible reply.

"We're having the most delightful conversation," Susan explained brightly. "He's a reporter for *Investor's Business Journal* and he heard about the accident and brought me some beautiful tulips."

Dean's eyes narrowed.

"Stay away from my..."

"Wife?" Warber supplied, regaining his composure and staring at Dean with a direct, cool challenge.

"I was going to say nanny," Dean grumbled.

"Nanny?" Susan repeated, her amber eyes widening in alarm.

Warber stood up and reached across the hospital bed to touch the frayed clasp of the suitcase Dean had found in Susan's room.

"Is that the pitiful little case that you're sending her away with?" he asked. "It breaks my heart."

"Sea slugs have no hearts."

"This one does."

Susan leaned forward.

"You're sending me away, darling? But why?"

Dean glowered at Warber, yanking the suitcase beyond the reporter's grasp.

"Get out of here," he said. "This is none of your business."

"Oh, but it is my business," Warber corrected. "My business is news—news of the financial world—and this particular domestic tragedy is most definitely news. My readers are going to want to know all about this."

"Save it for the tabloids. The business community isn't going to be interested in my problems."

"That's where you're wrong," Warber said defiantly. "The president of Radcliffe Enterprises is always news to the business community. And now that he's throwing his longtime nanny out on the streets just as she's recovering from…''

"Nanny?" Susan repeated more strongly.

"Wife," Warber conceded with a slight bow in Susan's direction. With growing courage, he corrected his potential article. "The president of Radcliffe throws his wife out on the streets after such a terrible accident."

"It's a rehab center," Dean said, barely controlling his anger at this intrusion. "She'll get some rest and come to her senses."

"Dean, what do I need a rehab center for?" Susan asked, her anxiety rising dramatically. "I want to go home to my children! Dr. Sugar said I could go home. Oooh, this talk makes my head hurt."

Both men looked at her with alarm as her hands pressed against her temple. She was clearly in pain, but as Dean rushed to her aid, she batted his hand away.

She wanted answers, not sympathy.

He backed off.

"It's a touching story," Warber said at last.

Dean whirled around.

"What do you want?" he demanded.

"I'm just looking for the human-interest angle."

"No! No! No! What is it that you really want?"

Warber opened his pink rosebud lips to launch an indignant protest about his journalistic integrity.

Then, reconsidering, he pressed his mouth into a tight, prim smile.

"I want an inside look at the negotiating process for Eastman Toys," he said in a snippy voice. "From a real insider's point of view."

"Fine," Dean spat out. "We'll arrange it."

"And I want—" Warber paused, measuring his advantage "—I want an exclusive. An interview with you. No-holds-barred."

"I never give interviews, and I especially don't give interviews to bottom-feeding sea slugs," Dean said adamantly, and then he glanced at Susan.

She had pulled her knees up to her chest and her shoulder blades stuck out vulnerably from her hospital gown.

He glared at Warber, who stepped back but held his eyes steady. Neither man was willing to back down.

A single teardrop of sweat coursed down Warber's forehead.

"All right, fine, you can have an interview with me." Dean surrendered. "Call Mrs. Witherspoon for an appointment. But wait a few hours, because if you call her before I get to her, she'll hang up on you so hard, you won't be able to hear for a week. She knows what kind of slime covers the ocean floor, and what kind of slime writes the news."

Warber opened his mouth, looking as if he might

ask for more or perhaps defend the honor of sea slugs everywhere. But Dean had had enough of the power of the press. His menacing stare was enough to cause Warber to nod a curt goodbye to Susan and hightail it out of the hospital room.

Now Dean's only problem was the woman lying on the bed. She regarded him from under thick, dark lashes.

He had never seen Susan looking so furious—on the other hand, he had never seen Susan at all. Had looked right through her.

But this new Susan was not the kind of woman a man could ignore.

"So, when did you start telling people I'm really your nanny?"

He swallowed. Hard.

Now was the time to tell her, to gently explain, to sympathize with her confusion and to send her on her way. His watch beeped three times, reminding him that he was supposed to be in a meeting. The quickest way to get out the door was to say yes and run.

Ungentlemanly, yes.

Smart, no doubt about it.

But there was something about her vulnerability, and the spunky tilt of her chin, or the painfully thin line of her shoulders.

Maybe it was her lips, trembling like the tenderest rosebuds before a subtle spring wind.

Those lips reminding him of their shared kiss.

Heaven help him, he shouldn't be noticing her this way!

And yet he put the suitcase on the floor and slid to the bed, sitting behind her.

"What do you think?" he whispered in her ear. "Do you think you're the nanny?"

"I think you're playing a terrible joke on me," she said, blinking back tears. "And I don't appreciate it. Not one little bit."

He pulled her into his embrace, meant to be comforting—though Dean was not normally a comforting kind of person. He held her closely and whispered to her that everything would be all right. Though he was the sort of realist who never tried to downplay a disaster.

He soothed her, though he wasn't a soothing man. Then his fingers caressed her fine, golden hair and he inhaled her sweet vanilla scent. His lips sought hers and then he caught himself.

"We'd better go," he said, pulling away.

"Home?" she asked. "Or to a rehab center for wayward nannies?"

He stood up and looked down at her, wondering what the harm would be to indulge her, to not prick any balloons or force her to acknowledge any hard truths—only until the nanny agency found her family.

And then he would make his apologies, sign

whatever checks were necessary to cover her care and be done. Because, by then, both of them would be embarrassed enough by their conduct to want escape.

It was folly, where his thoughts were leading. It was stupidity that would come back to haunt him, he was sure. He should turn this over to Mrs. Witherspoon, or to any of the other six hundred employees of the Radcliffe Enterprises. If he didn't have the courage to face those big amber golden eyes and tell her the truth, he should make someone else tell her.

Get her out of here, the voice of reason told him.

Send her away, his business sense commanded.

She waited for his answer with excruciating patience.

"Home," he conceded at last.

Her smile, warm and lush like the a spring garden, made him think that maybe, just maybe, he wasn't courting disaster.

Or, if he was, that it was worth it.

Chapter Six

The children raced ahead of her, chasing four spritely Monarch butterflies across the cobblestone courtyard. Susan hung back, tired but still steady on her flat sandals. Her breath came labored and hard.

But it was so good to be home!

In the scant two hours since Dean had brought her back, the children had ensured she didn't have a moment to sit down. And that's exactly the way she liked it.

Dr. Sugar had been so stern. Bed rest, plenty of fluids, pain medications if needed. The children had their own prescription in mind—their idea of doctor's orders involved running, playing, laughing and dancing.

She wouldn't trade this for a calm, relaxing instant in a rehab center. She crossed the courtyard in a half-dozen determined steps and sunk gratefully into the yellow-and-white cushions of the chaise.

"Give me just a minute to catch my breath!" she called out.

It was a perfect day—sunny and hot, but not too hot, with a gentle, green-scented breeze coming in from the lake. A perfect day to be alive. A perfect day for a smile, which now lit up Susan's face. A perfect day to come home from the hospital and see her children and remember all the reasons why she was glad to be who she was. It was a perfect day to be Susan Radcliffe—wife, mother and homemaker.

Admittedly, homemaker to the largest brick Georgian-style mansion in Winnetka. But a homemaker nonetheless. She kept an eye on the children while she planned dinner, thinking of the things she had found in the refrigerator and cupboards. Maybe spaghetti. The children loved spaghetti. And a steak for Dean. Rare. That's how he liked it. Funny how her memory was coming back in bits and pieces— she remembered all her husband's likes and dislikes, his quirks and habits. All her children's special qualities were coming back as well.

She glanced up at the house, noting the four second-floor windows that comprised her husband's study. He was working again, and acting most peculiar.

The former she had forgiven often in the course of her marriage, because she knew how important it was to Dean to meet new challenges. Even when they probably had enough money so that they could retire quite comfortably tomorrow if they wanted. But, of course, Dean wasn't thinking of retiring—and why should he when he was a strong, productive man at the peak of his business prowess?

But it was the latter of Dean's behavior—the acting peculiar—which gave her pause. The feather light lines of worry on her forehead deepened and her mouth tightened into an uncharacteristic frown.

He kept hinting, kept suggesting, kept trying to persuade her she was the children's nanny. Imagine that—some kind of private joke that she didn't appreciate. He'd spoken to her about it, had even brought to her hospital room a worn suitcase packed with clothes that he had claimed were hers. The clothes, hand mended and heartbreakingly old, had seemed familiar—carrying her scent and some of her style—and had made Susan quite uncomfortable.

She had put the suitcase in the empty guest room on the third floor when she returned from the hospital. She had then gone through her own closet for something to wear while playing with the children.

The clothes, hung on pink silk hangers in her

walk-in closet, had seemed oddly unfamiliar—
glitzy, and there were so many formal party dresses.
She couldn't remember having worn any of them.
At last she had grabbed a pale yellow sundress
shoved haphazardly on a wire hanger in the back
of a pile of sweaters. The sundress was more her
style.

The children had played along with Dean's joke.
And then they quickly saw that she was not amused
by it.

She was Mom.

And she wasn't the up-to-the-minute modern
kind of mom who wanted her children to call her
by her first name.

"Su—I mean, Mom—" Chelsea called. "Come
on, the butterflies are heading for the orchard!"

Susan stretched her weary body up, but was cut
short by two strong, muscular arms that clamped
down on the armrests on either side of her. Pinning
her down. She looked up into the strong, determined face that blocked the sun's light.

"You're not going anywhere," Dean said. "Dr.
Sugar prescribed rest—and running after those three
doesn't qualify as rest."

"The last thing I need is a break from the children," she said, arching forward so that her breasts
strained against the sundress's crinkled cotton.
"But if you'd like to carry me upstairs…?"

It was a bold and indecent invitation, but utterly

proper for a wife to make to her husband. And what a delicious proposition it was. Dean worked so hard that afternoons together were as rare as black pearls.

If they slipped upstairs now it would be scandalous, naughty, daring—and perfectly in keeping with her wedding vows.

"Upstairs?" he asked blankly.

"Sure," she said, allowing her eyes to linger at the hard need straining his jeans. "Dr. Sugar did say bed rest, didn't he? So how about carrying me up to bed?"

"Absolutely not!" he said abruptly, standing up straight and turning his broad back on her.

"Oh, Dean, why not?" she asked, ignoring the crisp and fleeting headache pain as she bolted upright. "We could ask Chelsea to play with the boys here in the garden, make them promise not to run off, and, of course, we'd leave the window in the bedroom open so we could hear if there was the slightest problem—"

"No, no, no!" he exclaimed, and though he barely moved out of her reach, Susan felt as stung as if he had slapped her hand away.

Dean was a man of physical needs.

She could hardly imagine him passing up the chance.

Still, she'd give it one more try. She came up behind him.

"I'm your wife," she reminded him, tracing a lazy pattern on his back, the muscles beneath her fingertips coiling with tension. She drawled sweetly, "I have a right to do this, Mr. Radcliffe. A right given to me by the state of Illinois for this express purpose."

He whirled around, and for the first time since their marriage she felt a smidgen of fear at the dark flame burning within his emerald eyes.

"I'm not your husband!"

"You've brought me into your house as your wife!" she lashed back at him.

"Maybe that was my mistake."

Anger ripped through her.

"A mistake? Our marriage is a mistake?"

"No, no. I mean, I'm not talking about that."

"Maybe you want to tell those three children out there that they're mistakes, too."

"No, Susan, no, never. They were never mistakes. And, I'm sorry, I shouldn't have said bringing you here was a mistake."

"Those children call me Mom. And they seem to think you're their father."

"Those children love their nanny so much that they're calling you Mom against my specific instructions!"

They stared at each other. His eyes were like burning gems.

She shivered, though it was not cold.

And instantly he softened, bringing her into a comforting, yet still oddly distant, embrace.

"I'm sorry," he said. "I have to remember you've been through so much in the past two days. And that I'm grateful for what you went through for those children."

She let her head fall to the swell of his chest. He stiffened for only a moment before pulling her to him. He couldn't feel this way, this perfect, this much a part of herself if he wasn't her husband.

"Oh, Susan." He sighed.

"Why do you have this silly idea I'm a nanny?" Susan asked dismally, feeling as if the world had been turned upside down.

He held her away from him and searched her face.

"It's not silly," he said at last. "I'm being perfectly rational."

"You're always very rational. But, in this case, you're also being silly."

"But I'm not! Susan, think carefully. Do you remember being my wife? Do you remember anything at all?"

Susan pulled away from him and walked to the edge of the border of hostas and lilies of the valley. She tossed her head, her golden hair rippling in the sunlight, and she regarded him from under lush eyelashes.

"I don't remember much of anything because my

head feels pretty muddled," she said defiantly. "But Dr. Sugar said that's perfectly understandable. It will all come back."

"Susan, what do you remember about our marriage, about us?"

"I remember a lot, a lot that a nanny wouldn't remember," she added pointedly. "Intimate things. Bedroom things. You-and-me things. Not just nanny things. You take me upstairs to that bedroom and I'll prove to you once and for all that I'm your wife. I'll prove to you that I remember the most important things about being your wife."

She turned to face him and he flushed red.

"I remember your kisses and...a whole lot more," Susan said, softening. "You're a deeply sensual man, a man who's very confident and powerful in bed. You're my husband and I've never known any other man. You taught me to be a woman. I am your woman. And all I'm asking you to do is go upstairs with me and let me prove it."

"You must have had a huge crush on me," he said, putting his face in his hands. "You poor girl. Out here at the house alone, without any friends, and I never noticed how terribly lonely you must have been. And how you must have developed some kind of infatuation for me. A simple crush, that's what this is."

"I do have a crush on you, a terrible one," she conceded. "I always have. That's why I married you. Here's how I can prove to you that I'm your wife if you won't go upstairs with me.''

"How?'' he asked warily.

"We'll ask Mr. Warber tonight. He's an objective third party.''

The look of horror on Dean's face nearly made Susan laugh aloud.

"Mr. Warber?''

"He's coming to dinner tonight,'' Susan said lightly. "He called to say that Mrs. Witherspoon hung up on him when he phoned for an interview, and I knew you wouldn't want that sort of rudeness tolerated, so I invited him for dinner and told him I'd leave you two alone in the study after we ate so you could talk.''

Dean slammed his fist into the brick wall bordering the garden. His knuckles were scraped raw, but he barely felt the pain.

"Mrs. Witherspoon! I forgot to call her to warn her that I'd agreed to see Warber,'' he groaned. "What am I going to do?''

"Simple,'' Susan said, as the children ran up the path from the orchard. "You're going to have dinner. And we'll ask Mr. Warber if I'm Mrs. Radcliffe. If he says I am Mrs. Radcliffe, I don't want to hear another word on the subject.''

She walked out onto the formal garden path, tossing her head lightly.

"One other thing, husband of mine.''

"What?"

"If he confirms that I am the nanny, I shall sleep in the upstairs quarters where that sorry excuse for a suitcase came from. However, if he says I am your wife, I will expect you to be in our bed exactly one hour after he goes home."

"I would have to answer the question by referring to the facts," Warber began that night in answer to Susan's question. His glasses shone like two round coins in the light from the table's four matching candelabra. "News reports of the tragic car accident outside the Radcliffe estate two years ago make it virtually impossible..."

Dean saw his children's faces around the table instantly go long and sad. There was no doubt where this conversation was heading—to Nicole and her tragic, shocking death.

He couldn't allow that.

"I don't want to talk about that this evening," he said firmly.

"So this question is more parlor game than search for truth?" Warber asked.

"Oh, no," Susan said. "We want the truth. The absolute truth. We're simply asking you to put to rest Dean's delusion that I'm a nanny. Or my delusion that I'm his wife."

"I want her to see the truth without having my

children hurt by painful memories," Dean said tersely.

"All right, I get the picture," Warber said, glancing once around the table. "I shall put on my Sherlock Holmes hat."

The children clapped and squealed as he pantomimed putting a hat on. Susan laughed. Even Dean felt a smile steal across his face.

Warber stuck the handle of a spoon in his mouth as if it were a pipe and knit his brows together as if in fiercest, deepest thought.

"Now, it's elementary, my dear Radcliffe," he said, in an exaggerated English accent. "We shall examine the evidence. Evidence number one—Susan is called Mom by each of the children."

"She is our mom," Chelsea said earnestly. She winked at Susan, but because she was not very practiced at it, the wink became a blink.

Henry and Baby Edward nodded their agreement with their sister.

"She's our mom," Henry said.

"Mommy," Baby Edward corrected.

"They call her Mom against my express instructions," Dean pointed out. "And because of their loyalty to a very good nanny. I have always regarded Susan as a fine caretaker of the house and the children."

"I'll take that as a compliment," Susan said, reserving a slyly murderous glance for Dean.

"Still, there is more evidence," Warber said, silencing the table with a haughty lift of his hand. He puffed at his imaginary pipe.

Dean grimaced. Warber was clearly enjoying himself to the hilt, having gained entry to the Radcliffe home and having been put squarely in the middle of a delicious domestic situation. Dean could just imagine the articles Warber would write on the subject. Dean didn't care for his own reputation, hated the media, had long since given up thinking he could affect how others regarded him.

But he thought now of Susan. After this was all over, her memory restored, she would find the media spectacle deeply embarrassing. For reasons he couldn't understand, he felt the pain of that embarrassment more acutely than he had felt anything since his wife's death.

He wanted to lunge across the table, grab Warber by the neck and demand his solemn oath that none of this would ever hit the papers.

Jaded as he was to the media, he figured the reporter's promise might be worth...well, absolutely nothing.

Still, he leaned forward just enough so that no one else at the table would hear his words.

"We have an agreement, Warber," he said vehemently.

"I know," Warber said, showing surprising courage since most people frankly cowered under

Dean's command. He pulled his handkerchief from his suit coat pocket and wiped his forehead. "I'm not breaking my end of our agreement. Not a word of this in print. I'm getting an exclusive interview from you. But for the moment, I've been asked by my hostess to decide whether she's Mrs. Radcliffe."

"So you have," Susan said, putting her hand on Dean's arm. "Calm down, darling."

Grumbling, Dean leaned back in his chair. He didn't like this. Not one bit.

Especially the part about sleeping arrangements after the dinner's conclusion.

Dean had felt edgy and inexplicably unable to concentrate after Susan had laid down her demand to share his bed.

He'd have to be a gentleman, but he'd have to not upset her.

Definitely a no-win situation.

And Dean Radcliffe had succeeded in business precisely because no one had ever cornered him into a no-win situation.

Until Susan, that is.

"Let's continue looking at the evidence," Warber said, acknowledging the children's whoops of delight with a regal bow. "The children call her Mom, she's living in the house and she's seated at a place not normally reserved for nannies."

"Does that mean he thinks you're Mom?" Chelsea whispered.

"Shh, let him finish!" Henry cried.

The three children sat as still as statues, eyes widened and completely focused on Warber.

"She wears stylish clothes with the air of a woman who understands beauty," Warber continued, nodding at the gold lamé evening gown Susan had purchased from one of Winnetka's finest dress shops just before his arrival. "She is a gracious and beguiling hostess. She knew exactly where the silverware and plates were when she set the table."

"What's bee-guy-ling?" Henry asked.

"Shhh!" Chelsea hissed.

"She looks like she belongs here," Warber said.

"She does!" the children chorused.

"And, most persuasive of all," Warber concluded, dropping his pipe and looking once at Susan and then at Dean with a look of sudden and complete enlightenment. "Most persuasive of all, you look awfully good together."

Chapter Seven

After putting the children to bed with another episode of the continuing adventures of the Eastman bears, Susan slipped downstairs to make coffee for the men who had retired to the study. Although she had done her best to keep the cooking area clean while she'd prepared dinner, and Mr. Warber had helped clear the table, the kitchen still looked like a disaster area.

Dirty dishes, half-empty glasses and smudged silverware littered the counters. Greasy and sticky pots and pans were piled high in the sink. Beyond the kitchen door, she saw the dining room tablecloth had several unsightly gravy stains. Crumbs littered the tiger maple tile.

It was a daunting sight—she had a lot of work to do.

But Susan merely smiled. She liked the afterglow of a successful party, when she knew that everyone had had a good time.

I could have lost all this, she thought—but I didn't, and I am so grateful. She was happy to be home, and though she knew that ordinarily she wouldn't thrill to the sight of dirty dishes, at least she knew this as a sign that life would return to normal very soon.

She set up the coffeemaker, arranged a package of dainty gourmet chocolate cookies on a plate and picked out two matching sets of cups and saucers from the cabinet over the sink.

It crossed her mind that people of their means could well afford servants beyond the maid service that came twice a week to do the most onerous tasks. Somebody to wash the dishes even if Susan wanted to make the dinner. Somebody to iron the tablecloth even if Susan wanted to set the table. Somebody to take care of the children if she wanted to take a nap. But Susan knew she wouldn't have liked that, that she wanted to keep her hands on every home project and her feet firmly planted on the ground.

Her most important tasks were making a home for her husband and children. It was who she wanted to be—and while she admired those women who worked by choice or necessity, she knew that she wouldn't find her success in the workplace.

"I haven't forgotten you, Wiley," she said to the animal who had patiently waited in his corner of the kitchen. "Steak and carrots."

He licked once at her black peau de soie pumps in gratitude as she put down the bowl with the chopped-up leftovers. She patted him on the head, poured the hot coffee into a china pot and carried the tray into the study.

She was so glad to be back home.

Back to her normal life.

"Here, you shouldn't be doing that," Dean said, jumping to his feet and taking the tray from her. "Besides, Mr. Warber was just leaving."

"You were?" Susan asked, puzzled. "I thought you were going to give him an extensive interview."

"I already have," Dean said firmly.

He glanced significantly at Warber, who scurried to pick up his notes, tape recorder and pencils.

"Yes, that's right, I'm done."

Warber's courage seemed to have lasted only until dessert.

Or until he was alone with Dean.

"I'm sorry I missed it," Susan said, sitting casually on the upholstered arm of Dean's chair. "The children love the Eastman toy bears so much, and soon Dean will be the president of that company. I can't wait to see how he'll make our favorite bears even better.''

"But that's not exactly what he has planned," Warber said.

A sudden chill descended on the room as Warber looked up at Dean. Susan followed his gaze and was stunned to see Dean's returning glare. Dean looked utterly without emotion, and yet so strong and potent that only a fool would cross him now.

And Warber, at her side, seemed to quiver with the certainty that he had just provoked Dean.

But Susan knew Dean, had always felt that she could see beyond the public mask he presented, could see into his heart and understand him. What she saw now was a fury that Warber rightfully should fear. She also saw, quite clearly, that he hadn't told her about his plans for the Eastman Bear Company because he knew it wouldn't please her. Wouldn't please her a bit.

One thing she knew about her husband: he wanted to please her. He always wanted to please the people he loved.

She placed a comforting arm on his shoulder— really a restraining arm, though Dean was never a violent man.

He might scare Warber, but he wouldn't lay a hand on him.

Still, curiosity got the better of her role as peacemaker.

"Darling, what is it that you have planned for the company?" she asked.

Dean glanced at her, but his words were directed at Warber.

"I'm breaking it apart," he said stiffly. "The land that the factory sits on is more valuable than the going concern—and no amount of cash put into the company's hands is going to change that. It's a company run by people with bear fantasies and not business facts."

Susan's heart charged.

"Why, Dean, you can't do that! The children love the Eastman bears! They're wonderful teddy bears, with real personalities. That's a small business that needs your help. You've rescued other companies. Why can't you do that here?"

It wasn't until Dean yanked his rumpled sleeve back from her grasp that she realized how intensely she had reacted. Warber mumbled something about having enjoyed their hospitality but that he really must be going.

"Yes, you really should," Dean said with bare civility. "Let me escort you to the door."

Susan would have followed—it was rude to not at least see her dinner guest to the door—but she felt a sudden dizziness. Dr. Sugar had warned her about overdoing things, especially the first few days home from the hospital. And here she was—not twelve hours after having come home—with a dinner party concluded, the children put to bed and the shock of learning her husband was destroying a company that produced her children's favorite toys.

Worse was her husband acting in such a callous and cold manner.

She settled like a puddle into one of the wing chairs positioned at the side of the fireplace. She listened as Dean walked Warber to the front foyer.

"I'm warning you, Warber," Dean said. "I don't want a word about Susan in print. And that business of telling her she was my wife—you shouldn't confuse and encourage her."

"You could solve the whole problem by laying out the truth about—"

"No, I won't," Dean said harshly. "I can't. And you won't, either."

The two men's voices grew low, too low for Susan to hear.

The truth? She puzzled for a moment, but it hurt too much to think.

She leaned back in the chair and closed her eyes.

A minute later, she heard the door slam shut and her husband's footsteps returning down the hallway to the study. She looked up at him as he entered.

"Susan, are you all right?" he demanded, crouching down at her side. "You look pale."

"Just a little…little weak," she admitted.

"You've overdone it," Dean said. "Coming home from the hospital, cooking a five-course dinner, playing with the kids. I can't believe I've allowed you to push yourself. Tomorrow you'll stay in bed. All day. I'll hire someone to come in and take care of the house and the kids."

"No!" Susan cried. "I don't want anyone else in my house. I'm fine and I'll be even better tomorrow. I played with the children today because I love them and I entertained for Mr. Warber because I love you. It's who I am as a wife and a mother. I love you, Dean."

He flinched as her words crescendoed to a nearly frantic conclusion. Without another word, he stood and walked to the window, looking out onto the moonlit courtyard.

Susan twisted her wedding ring nervously.

"Don't take apart that company. Don't buy it just to sell it off in pieces."

"Susan, that's a business decision, not an emotional one."

"Please, Dean, do it for the children."

"They don't need it."

"They do. And if you don't believe me, then do it for me. Do it for me."

He turned away.

"Is there something you're not telling me, Dean?" she asked softly. "Perhaps you don't love me anymore? Is that it?"

He whirled around and strode across the study to pick her up into his arms. She thrilled to his touch, assuming it would be followed by a powerful, lust-driven kiss.

Instead, he commanded she look at him.

"Susan, I can't say I love you, because you're not the woman you think you are!" he said, shaking her to emphasize his words. He released her when he realized what he was doing.

She didn't budge, standing toe to toe to him, refusing to back down to her husband.

A husband who was suffering from a most bizarre delusion—the delusion that his wife was really a delusional nanny.

"It's that nanny thing again."

"Yes."

"I thought we settled that."

"We didn't. Warber was just playing."

"The children think I'm your wife. The doctors at the hospital thought I was your wife. Warber thinks I'm your wife. What more do you want before you stop torturing me with this silly idea?"

She covered her face with her hands, and he rushed to comfort her.

"Susan, sit down. I'm sorry I brought it up again. But when you ask me if I love you, I have to talk about it."

"What if I asked you to kiss me?" Susan asked, pulling her hands away from her face and looking at him, daring him, with the calmest expression she could muster. "What if I, this mousy nanny you describe, asked you to make love to me right now, the way a husband would? What if the nanny asked you to take me up to our bed. Our bed, Dean. If you wanted to pretend I'm the nanny, I guess I'm just enough of an adventurer that I'd be willing to try it that way. So what do you say, Mr. Radcliffe?''

"I would want to, I'd really want to," he said. "But I wouldn't. Because you're my children's nanny and I'd be taking advantage of you."

"How can I prove once and for all I'm your wife?" Susan screamed.

Her outburst startled them both. Feeling a hot blush of embarrassment, Susan glanced up at the ceiling, wondering if she had woken the children. But there was not a sound.

"All right," Dean said, struggling to keep his calm. "Let me just ask you a few questions. I'm sure you'll discover that you're not my wife. What was our wedding like?"

Susan closed her eyes, trying to conjure in the darkness an image. An image of their wedding.

"I wore white," she guessed.

"Everyone does."

"There were flowers?"

"Everyone has flowers at their wedding."

"There was cake."

"Susan, you're grasping at straws."

"You wore a tux."

"So far, Susan, you haven't said anything that couldn't be said about a thousand different weddings."

"It's a little muddled in my head," Susan admitted. "But maybe it's part of the recovery problems Dr. Sugar warned about. Or maybe it's simply because the best weddings leave a bride in a daze. Ask me another question."

He regarded her carefully.

"Why'd we get married?"

"Because we love each other," she said, without hesitation.

"Why do I love you?" he asked, truly puzzled. After all, so much of his heart had felt dead in the past two years....

She stared at him hard.

"Because I'm charming, nice, have a terrific personality and look a lot better than Wiley in a dress," she said dryly.

At least he had the decency to flush bright red.

"I'm sorry. That was an ungentlemanly question. How about if you answer the other one?"

"What other one?"

He hesitated. And she saw inside of him the doubts that no one else could see, the insecurities that were hidden by a mantle of power and determination, the loneliness that was covered by masculine charisma.

"Oh, you mean why I love you," she supplied. "That's an easy one to answer."

"It is?"

"Sure," she said, rising to his arms. She playfully batted away his hands as he protested. She arched her back to close the distance between their mouths. Her breath touched his face with a glittering fresh sensation and then her lips brushed against his. Before he could pull away, she plunged her tongue into his mouth—teasing and taunting the tip of his flesh.

He had taught her how he liked it, so long ago, she thought.

And she had remembered every lesson he gave in the art of lovemaking.

The silence between them was broken by her insistent heartbeat.

He rewarded her with an instinctive press of his hips. His own needs exploded; he opened her mouth with his own tongue and soon it wasn't Susan who demanded so much from their kiss. He kissed her as a man would, a fully male invitation to them both.

Suddenly she pulled away, having awakened to his raw masculinity. And, though he clearly had the power—and the hardened need—to bring her back to him, he let her go. He must have seen the fear in her eyes.

And yet, she was his wife.

She shouldn't fear the lovemaking that followed such intense kissing.

She had been married to Dean for years.

So why would she feel this way, as if she didn't know what to expect?

Fear mingled with desire—too intense for her to bear.

Maybe she needed to take it more slowly.

"Why'd you stop?" he asked huskily.

"Because there's more time," she answered with a determined wifely playfulness that was tempered by her body's trembling. "Because there's so much more time to take it slow. We have all night, Dean. That's the point of being married."

She opened the french doors that looked out over the courtyard, then found the Harry Connick, Jr. CD she was looking for and turned on the stereo. As the first strains of the music began, she held her hand out to Dean. Puzzled, he followed her out the glass doors.

The light was moonlight. The perfume was lilies of the valley from the garden. The night was warm, but not too warm. The music was dancing and romancing music. She came into his arms and she felt first the recoiling and then the precious surrender as his arms took her.

She was relieved in some small way that his aching need did not press itself against her. Instead, he held her at a distance that was both intimate and yet not explicitly sexual. Odd for him to be such a gentleman. But she was grateful.

Dancing was nice, dancing was safe, dancing would help her regain her balance.

"This is why I married you," she whispered in his ear. "Because, Dean Radcliffe, you are definitely the best dancer I know."

Chapter Eight

It was too much for even the strongest, most honorable man.

A moonlit night, an empty cobblestone courtyard, romantic jazz music filtering out of the open study doors and a beautiful woman with open, inviting eyes, pressing herself against him in a perfectly proper, but oh-so-seductive tease.

"Susan, I don't think this is a very good idea," Dean said uneasily, trying to keep her at arm's length.

"Why?" she asked playfully, laughing as she drew even closer to him. "I love to dance. I always have. And you did ask me to tell you why I married you. Even you must remember this part of our wedding. I remember this part very well. We danced.

And danced. Oh, I loved to dance with you. I still do."

Actually, the idea of the ever-sensible nanny Susan loving to dance was patently ridiculous.

To begin with, his children's nanny would never undulate against him in such a sensual manner—though he admitted to himself that she remained on the strictly correct side of the boundary of propriety while still driving his baser animal nature to distraction. He had forgotten a woman could do that to him.

And secondly, his children's nanny would never, ever sway so gracefully, the silk of her gold lamé gown caressing his legs, her movements hinting at the flesh beneath its pleated folds. Susan the nanny had been very good at hauling several children, or laundry baskets, from point A to point B—and Dean was sure he hadn't noticed any particular grace or charm in her movements. Or maybe he hadn't been watching carefully enough.

Third, the Susan he knew, or at least had employed for the past year, would never, ever dance when there were dirty dinner dishes soaking in the kitchen sink.

But, most importantly of all, his children's nanny would never enjoy herself so much.

This couldn't possibly be his Susan dancing with him! And if it wasn't her, then he wasn't bound by any protective impulse. He could kiss her, reach

Play "Lucky Hearts" and you get.

YOURS FREE!

This lovely necklace will add glamour to your most elegant outfit. Its cobra-link chain is a generous 18" long, and its lustrous simulated cultured pearl is mounted in an attractive pendant! Best of all, it's ABSOLUTELY FREE, just for accepting our NO-RISK offer.

...then continue your lucky streak with a sweetheart of a deal!

1. Play Lucky Hearts as instructed on the opposite page.

2. Send back this card and you'll receive brand-new Silhouette Romance™ novels. These books have a cover price of $3.25 each, but they are yours to keep absolutely free.

3. There's no catch. You're under no obligation to buy anything. We charge nothing—ZERO—for your first shipment. And you don't have to make any minimum number of purchases—not even one!

4. The fact is thousands of readers enjoy receiving books by mail from the Silhouette Reader Service™. They like the convenience of home delivery...they like getting the best new novels BEFORE they're available in stores...and they love our discount prices!

5. We hope that after receiving your free books you'll want to remain a subscriber. But the choice is yours—to continue or cancel, any time at all! So why not take us up on our invitation, with no risk of any kind. You'll be glad you did!

◆ **Exciting Silhouette romance novels—FREE!**
◆ **Plus a lovely Simulated Pearl Drop Necklace—FREE!**

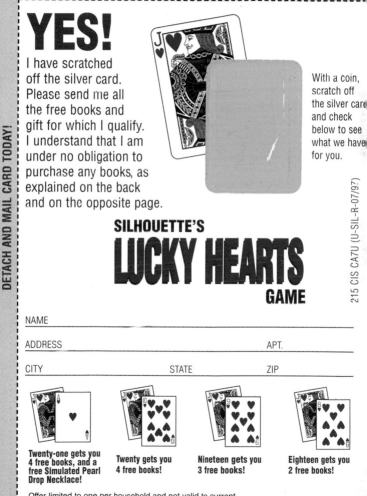

The Silhouette Reader Service™—Here's how it works:

Accepting free books places you under no obligation to buy anything. You may keep the books and gift and return the shipping statement marked "cancel." If you do not cancel, about a month later we'll send you 6 additional novels and bill you just $2.67 each plus 25¢ delivery per book and applicable sales tax, if any.* That's the complete price—and compared to cover prices of $3.25 each—quite a bargain! You may cancel at any time, but if you choose to continue, every month we'll send you 6 more books, which you may either purchase at the discount price...or return to us and cancel your subscription.
*Terms and prices subject to change without notice. Sales tax applicable in N.Y.

If offer card is missing write to: Silhouette Reader Service, 3010 Walden Ave., P.O. Box 1867, Buffalo, NY 14240-18

BUSINESS REPLY MAIL
FIRST-CLASS MAIL   PERMIT NO. 717   BUFFALO, NY

POSTAGE WILL BE PAID BY ADDRESSEE

SILHOUETTE READER SERVICE
3010 WALDEN AVE
PO BOX 1867
BUFFALO NY 14240-9952

NO POSTAGE
NECESSARY
IF MAILED
IN THE
UNITED STATES

down to touch her lips as if she truly were his wife....

"Susan, I can't do this," he said, extricating his arms and holding her away from him. The scent of vanilla and something delicately floral receded, leaving him with a sharp, acute longing that was rivaled only by his shock at his own impulsive actions.

If he didn't get a hold of himself right now...

She looked up at him with glistening round, amber eyes.

"Please," she said simply, her lower lip trembling.

He couldn't refuse. He couldn't resist.

It was dancing, just dancing.

What could be the harm?

As he swept her around the cobblestone courtyard, he rationalized that he was doing her a favor. Dancing didn't mean he was taking advantage of her, and he wasn't upsetting her, as he had done this evening. Even with his arms around her, he could still think of himself as a gentleman so long as he kept her twirling around the cobblestones. Although that particular description of himself—gentleman—wasn't something he had ever given much thought to before.

Her situation, the very vulnerability of a woman whose strength and sensibilities he had taken for granted, made him a gentleman.

For the first time in so long.

As the music slowed, her head snuggled against his neck. He looked up at the moon and the stars twinkling through the tall oak leaves. It was a clear, perfect night. She felt so wonderful in his arms.

He was doing the right thing, he was sure.

This turn around the courtyard would hardly add much to the sum total of foolish things she had done since the accident. Giving dinner parties, the children calling her Mom, calling him her husband, kissing him…again and again. Dancing with him would be just one more embarrassment when she discovered who she was.

She'd be so red in the face, she'd never want to speak to him again, if he knew his children's nanny as he thought he did. She'd quit her job rather than face him again—and that would be for the best.

For both of them.

He groaned at the delicious lingering pleasure, looked up at the twinkling stars beyond the oaks and then caught himself, remembering that he wasn't supposed to be enjoying himself.

"Happy, darling?" she asked him as the music stopped between songs.

"Yes, I hadn't thought about it, but I guess I am," he answered cautiously.

It wasn't a question that anyone—including himself—had asked in a very long time.

"I'm so very happy, too," she said, looking up at him, her face glowing in the moonlight.

And that's when Dean confessed the truth—to himself if not to her.

He was dancing with her because he wanted to.

Just because he wanted to.

Because he wanted to feel her in his arms. It had been too long since he felt a woman's body pressed against him. He briefly thought of the heartache of the past years, the events leading up to Nicole's accident and the shattering finality of her death.

But he pushed those dark thoughts roughly aside because this moment was what was important, even if Susan was a troubled young nanny. Even if he was a foolish and lonely man.

He was with a beautiful woman and she wanted to dance.

And a real gentleman never refused a lady's request to dance. Nothing could be more delicious than holding her in his arms.

They danced the slow dances and the faster ones. Dean had learned the steps as an eighth grader, forced by his parents to take ballroom dancing classes, but where Susan had learned to dance he didn't know. When he asked her, she simply laughed.

"I don't really know how to dance at all," she said gaily. "I'm just following you. We're good together."

At that moment, Harry Connick, Jr. finished the last of his jazzy love tunes. The courtyard fell silent. She looked up at him, her hands skittering nervously across his chest.

Now was the time, he thought.

The time to kiss her. The moment she expected it.

A natural conclusion to an evening of dancing.

A natural beginning to a night of...

He touched his index finger against her lower lip in a warning, as she stared at him. Waiting. She didn't pull away, but stared at him with eyes of liquid gold. He closed his eyes against the rising tide of desire, the tug at his gabardine pants that expressed his wants, the quickening of his heartbeat that signaled his needs.

He shouldn't want her, didn't want her, couldn't want sensible, no-nonsense, plain, ordinary Susan.

Before this week, he reminded himself, he hadn't taken the slightest notice of her. And now he thought she was the most beautiful, delicate flower of a woman. She reached up on her tiptoes and brushed her lips lightly against his. A feather-soft invitation. Her breath touched his face with glittering warmth. She was poised to surrender to him.

She thought she was his wife, that she should have no fear of the sensual unknown. Still, as he rested his finger at the base of her neck, he felt her pulse race beneath the silky skin. She was afraid,

afraid of making love to a man for the first time, perhaps for the first time ever. And yet, unaware of her own inexperience.

"Do you know what you're asking for?" he wondered aloud.

"Yes," she answered hesitantly. "I don't remember...I don't remember everything. But I want you to come to bed. I want us to be man and wife again."

He stood as woodenly as the cherub that guarded the fountain at the courtyard's center. His own blood tormented him, coursing through him with intense, primitive desire. He felt the straining at his groin and the reckless tremor of his hands as they ached to take her, to make her his own. But he didn't move. He waited.

At last she fell back on her heels, her eyes downcast, her lashes casting a long dark shadow across her scarlet cheeks.

"I really better get back to work," he said softly.

"Do you have to?" she asked, and he knew that it cost her pride to ask.

Still, he couldn't give in.

"Yes, I have to," he said abruptly. Wanting all the time to say "No, come to me, kiss me, promise me that you won't regret...anything."

"You'll come to bed later?" Her voice cracked.

"Yes," he answered softly, not wanting another

confrontation to ruin this special moment, wishing he could do as they both wanted.

But what they both wanted was wrong and only he knew it. He would have to be right—for both of them.

He relinquished her, and with a final, chaste kiss on her forehead, walked up the steps to the study door. He turned off the stereo, flipped on the desk lamp and stared for several minutes at the documents on the table before him.

He had enough work to keep him occupied for hours, and ordinarily that prospect would have energized him.

Instead, he restlessly paced over to the window, and watched as Susan picked up the folds of her long gown. Careful of her hem, she walked gracefully on the garden path toward the orchard. He would give anything to join her, and perhaps he could.

Who was to say that he couldn't? And when her memory returned, why couldn't he shush her embarrassment and make her his own? Men in his position had done worse, more foolish things, than marrying a woman like Susan.

But that fleeting prospect died even as he played out the possibilities. He thought of Nicole. The twisted body. The wrecked car. The children in hysterics. And he knew that something of himself had died that night with his wife. Some precious part of his heart that would never be reborn.

Even Susan couldn't repair that part of him.

I can't be the nanny, Susan thought as she looked back at the mansion from the cover of the orchard's trees.

"I can't be the nanny when I know my family so well," she said aloud. The words, once said, seemed even more true than when she thought them in the quiet of self-doubt.

She knew Chelsea liked to sew dresses for her dolls, was crushed when she wasn't invited to Nancy Smith's birthday party, had one baby tooth gone and three more loose. She knew Henry wanted to be Batman, got too punchy when frustrated and didn't like to have his ears cleaned. She knew Baby Edward was scared of the dark, sometimes sucked his Eastman teddy's ear when he was going to sleep and took cookies from the jar when he thought no one was looking.

And she knew her own house; she hadn't hesitated a moment when selecting the plates, linens, silverware and crystal goblets for the dinner party. Knew where the extra bottle of Chardonnay wine was kept. Knew that Chelsea would eat her Tater Tots, but Henry would disdain them. Knew Baby Edward liked his carrots cut up very fine.

And most of all, she knew her husband. Knew

his drive to succeed, to go beyond what his own father had accomplished in the business world. She knew Dean's hardness, the core within him that measured him against an unreachable standard. She knew his needs, knew that when he wanted a woman, he wanted to possess her totally, to take from her every possible pleasure and go beyond every boundary of propriety.

So what had those kisses meant? The light ones, soft and gentle like a baby's? He was holding back so much of his masculine power and ardor—didn't he want her anymore? Or was he frightened of hurting her, as if the lightning had made her too delicate for his touch?

Still, she had felt fear—a tiny pinprick of fear—when she had thought they were at last going upstairs to their bed. Why should she fear the man who knew her body as his own and whose body in turn was pledged to her for life?

She pondered this as she walked back to the house, pausing once at the courtyard to look into the study window. The desk lamp was on, casting the silhouette of his face. He was working again. Worked too much, really.

She cleaned up the kitchen and went upstairs.

Sometimes he hid in his work, using the excuses of the business world to shield him from the emotions he couldn't control, couldn't command.

If she didn't do something about this breach between them, this small tear in their marriage would never heal. She didn't want him to think of her as too fragile. She didn't want him to retreat into his world of work. She loved him and she wouldn't lose him.

She resolved to do everything in her power to show him that she was the wife she had always been. A good mother. A good homemaker. A good friend.

And, most of all, a good lover.

She would win back all of her husband's affections, and as she undressed and slipped into the king-size bed she shared with him, not once did it cross her mind that she didn't belong between the finely embroidered Egyptian cotton sheets.

Later, after midnight, Dean rubbed his eyes and switched off the study light. He stretched and walked into the spotless kitchen for a glass of water. Hard to believe there had been a dinner party here, harder still to believe that he had danced with Susan in the courtyard just beyond the window.

He walked upstairs, flicked on the bedroom light, startled, and then stared at Susan, who was sleeping on one side of the giant bed. Her golden hair fanned out on the pillow, her breasts strained against the sheets.

He couldn't sleep next to her. That was out of the question, regardless of the wager he had lost.

Warber may have said they looked good together but that was no reason for him to slip between the sheets with Susan.

He should turn around and walk down the hall to the guest suite. But then he looked at the pristine shape of the bed on her other side and reconsidered. She was too smart. She'd know if he never came to this bed.

He'd lay down for a minute, he thought, watching her as he undressed. When he was stripped of all but his white boxer briefs, he carefully eased back the sheets on the side of the bed beside her. He lay down. He tossed and turned and pounded his head backward on the pillow.

There. Rumpled as all get-out.

He could now go to the guest bed, set the alarm for early, and let her just think he had risen before her.

He didn't know why he wanted to protect her illusion, but somehow he knew that it was useless to keep repeating the truth. She simply wasn't going to believe him. But she'd remember the truth eventually. Susan would become the nanny once more— soon enough.

A call today to the nanny agency had confirmed that they were working on locating her file. And, as soon as they did, a family would appear. Her memory would return. She would go back to wherever she had come from. He would miss her, but having dealt with loss so many times, he knew he would get over her.

He'd have to.

Just as he was easing out of the bed, she rolled over. Dean froze. Had he woke her?

No, her breathing was heavy and even. He was safe. He pushed the sheet back.

She turned again, this time snuggling up under his arm, laying her head on his shoulder. It felt so natural that for a bare instant he forgot himself. And inhaled the warm, now familiar, scent. And caressed the corn-silk soft hair.

He felt her silky leg cover his own.

And he realized that he was trapped.

Trapped until morning.

Chapter Nine

Shocked into utter silence, Dean stared across his desk at Mrs. Witherspoon. She was crying. Mrs. Witherspoon never cried, and certainly never created a ruckus.

Now she was doing both, sobbing with wracking shudders punctuated by wheezing gasps that made him think she was going to stop breathing altogether. But, just as he thought he might have to call 911, she'd heave a great sigh and begin the crying anew.

Dean heard her phone ringing at the neat little desk where she normally, until this very moment, served as the gatekeeper to his office.

He discreetly turned his wrist so that he could peek at his watch. Seven o'clock. The receptionist wasn't in to reroute the call.

Just when he thought he couldn't bear listening to it any longer, the phone stopped ringing.

Mrs. Witherspoon, having worked at that desk for him and his father before him, had taken care of every detail that might distract the father and son from the most essential demands of Radcliffe Enterprises. Dean could not imagine a workday without the efficient and capable Mrs. Witherspoon at his side. That's why he had included her in profit sharing the very day he took over the business.

Seeming to work twenty-four hours a day, she was as unnoticed and as utterly essential in her sphere as Susan was in his house.

Until Susan had turned into his...bed mate.

He let his mind wander briefly to the memory of awakening this morning, her head still on his shoulder, her scent mingled with his, her arm draped lightly across his bare chest. It had been positively indecent and had immediately provoked a physical need that was hard and unrepentant.

He had slipped out of her arms, dressed quickly and had driven to the office, though there wasn't much to be done that he hadn't already taken care of the night before in his study.

But staying in bed with a nearly naked woman who thought she was his wife and who made him feel like a teen in the clutches of hormones would have been more than he could have resisted!

And now, no sooner had he walked into the office, than he found Mrs. Witherspoon sobbing over the day's *Investor's Business Journal* and wielding it over his desk like some kind of sword. What was she shrieking?

"I'm quitting! I'm quitting!" Mrs. Witherspoon sobbed into her linen handkerchief. "I can't take what you're doing. Look at this thing!"

She dumped the paper on his desk and he skimmed the headlines on the front page.

An article on recent investment opportunities in Peruvian copper mining.

An editorial about pending legislation to regulate the production and distribution of cotton in the Southeastern United States.

A report on the plans for the Radcliffe purchase of the Eastman Bear Company.

Here Dean's eyes narrowed. Warber had been busy after the dinner party. Must have gone straight to the office. Must have held the presses for the article.

He scanned the text quickly and, though he hadn't the chance to read every word and digest every nuance to the article, he nonetheless silently gave the reporter credit where credit was most definitely due.

The article didn't mention Susan.

And, frankly, Dean didn't care what Warber wrote about so long as he didn't write about Susan.

So Warber had acted like a gentleman after all.

Dean opened his mouth, about to tell Mrs. Witherspoon to dial the journal and get Warber on the line to say thank you. Then he decided against it. She was in no condition to be placing calls.

But why should yet another article about Radcliffe Enterprises be so upsetting to Mrs. Witherspoon? After all, she kept a file folder in her desk where she dropped every press mention of Radcliffe Enterprises during the month. By the twentieth of every month, that file folder was always bulging.

And she always exhibited pride over each mention.

"I assume you're not troubled by the Peruvians or the cotton regulations?" Dean asked. "It's the Warber article, right?"

Mrs. Witherspoon stared heavenward, counting to ten.

When she was done, she looked at him with a fury that was quiet, but not one whit less forceful.

"You're buying Eastman Bear Company for its land value, aren't you?"

"Yes, I am," he said and he let his eyes drift to the sun-sparkled lake beyond the floor-to-ceiling windows lining the eastern wall of his office. He had been so focused on protecting Susan from scandal, he hadn't considered the effect of an article on the merger. "I suppose this complicates the negotiations a little if the company president knows this in advance, but I'm still pretty optimistic that we'll be able to conclude the deal, sell the factory and the land within the next month.''

''That's terrible!''

''But, Mrs. Witherspoon, you knew we were negotiating for this sale. You've been working on the paperwork for ages.''

''But you didn't tell me you were buying it for its land value,'' she snapped.

''You'll get a tidy bonus check in your monthly envelope,'' he said, thinking perhaps she had thought he wouldn't remember. ''We always do that when Radcliffe makes a profitable deal. And don't worry, Mrs. Witherspoon, this deal will be very profitable.''

''Well, this month, I don't want that blood money!'' Mrs. Witherspoon declared. ''I'm quitting!''

And, without another word, she left, picking up her purse from her desk on the way out. He knew she meant business because the phone rang seven times and she didn't slow her step a bit.

''Mrs. Witherspoon!'' he called, running after her when he realized she wasn't coming back.

But she was already in an elevator—heading down.

He raked his fingers through his hair. He was certain she'd come back. She'd have to come back. He'd persuade her to come back. No one had ever resisted him for long. He went back to his desk and read the article more carefully.

It was straightforward, no-nonsense, with not a single misquote. Warber dutifully tracked Dean's father as a titan of business, but made clear that Dean had taken Radcliffe Enterprises further than anyone could ever have imagined, that the workplace environment he had created was intense, that Dean's ability to spot trends in business and finance was renown, that several companies had been brought back from the edge of financial ruin through his intervention, that for all his reputation as a tough businessman, Dean had saved many Americans their jobs and their savings.

Warber even put in a pitch about how Dean had financed much of the Winnetka Community Hospital's new critical-care unit. As he read, Dean winced with embarrassment at the praise, but recognized that this kind of masterfully subtle publicity was the only way that other charitably minded people would pull out their checkbooks.

All in all a fine article, Dean thought as he put the paper back on the desk. After rereading twice the final two paragraphs about the Eastman Bear Company, he hadn't a clue why Mrs. Witherspoon should find the deal so upsetting.

She couldn't quit, he thought as he noticed the urgently ringing phones. He was stretched to the breaking point as it was. He needed her.

He walked out to her abandoned desk. The extrawide phone had five lights blinking furiously. He looked out to the hallway of offices with clerical cubicles in front of each door. No one was here yet. A fax machine buzzed furiously and began blurting out paper.

Then he remembered—he had decided Mrs. Witherspoon would spend the day at the house, taking care of Susan. Or, more precisely, taking care that Susan wouldn't get into trouble.

He gingerly picked up the receiver on Mrs. Witherspoon's phone and punched in the first line.

"Radcliffe," he growled.

"This is Buster Milbert with the *Daily Chronicle*," a squeaky voice replied. "We're looking for some answers on the story of Mr. Radcliffe's wife being discharged from the hospital yesterday. Can we get a statement from Mr. Radcliffe?"

"No comment," Dean said, and hung up.

He grimly looked at the other blinking lights. Warber might have acted like a gentleman and kept Susan out of the limelight, but that didn't mean other reporters would feel the same way.

He answered seven other calls—three were other reporters from business-oriented columns who smelled a story, and three were from members of his negotiating team who were anxious to meet with Eastman and conclude the deal. One was the nanny agency, saying their staff was trying its best but

hadn't yet figured out where Susan's family was—
or even if any family existed. Dean responded to
that last call by making his own phone call to the
head of corporate security to put a private detective
on the case.

"Susan's family must be found," he said urgently, knowing that he couldn't possibly spend another night with her in his bed without surrendering
to his desires.

"I'll have something by tonight, boss."

With that pronouncement, Dean felt more confident.

He would be sending Susan home to her family
and himself back to his very ordinary routine by the
end of the day.

He was going to forget about Susan as surely as
she had forgotten about herself.

And he was going to do everything in his power
to get Mrs. Witherspoon back at her desk, but until
then he would manage. He called her house but
there was no answer.

At eight-thirty, he strode to the elevator bank,
nodding goodbye to the receptionist.

"I'll be at Eastman Bears with the rest of the
negotiating team," he said. "Mrs. Witherspoon
isn't...isn't here this morning, so take all my
calls."

He started to whistle a tune, stopping abruptly as

he realized it was the slow, dreamy melody to which he and Susan had danced.

And then the elevator doors opened.

He gasped and felt a swift choking sensation that tugged at his collar.

He looked down first at the three children coming out of the elevator. Chelsea, dressed in a pink sundress, carrying a beach ball. Henry wearing flippers and trunks, twirling a snorkel in his hand. Baby Edward sucking his thumb and clutching a rubber duck.

The three children were followed by a pair of long legs, draped in a black chiffon cover-up that teased and taunted his eyes.

His gaze traveled with instinctive appraisal from the siren-red polished toenails to the curvy calves to the tempting thighs and finally to the demure but oh-so-tempting black one-piece swimsuit.

Her smooth, pale skin glistened with the slightest blush of summer.

Her hair was pulled back into a sleek ponytail.

She was trouble and she had three little helpers.

"Hello, darling," Susan said, stepping out of the elevator and planting a wifely kiss on his cheek. "We're going to the beach and we were wondering if you'd like to join us."

Susan felt ridiculous wearing a swimsuit into an office building, even if it was her husband's office building and she was wearing a chiffon cover-up that, had it been made of more substantial fabric, could have served as a tent. Not only did she feel ridiculous, she felt humiliated—having to beg her husband to take a day off to be with her and the children.

But Susan was a determined woman, not easily daunted by an obstinant husband, and so she pleaded and begged and cajoled as Dean backpedaled away from her to his office.

"Just for one day," Susan cried. "We haven't spent much time together as a family and you need some time off. We need to be a family again and you're not doing your fair share. You're turning into a workaholic."

She grasped Baby Edward's hand because he was starting to sniffle—flat-out sobbing would set in in minutes. Chelsea and Henry trailed behind her, Chelsea muttering darkly that her father would never, ever, ever take a day off to be with them.

Chelsea looked like she might be right.

If Dean Radcliffe weren't her husband, Susan would turn right around and take these children home.

But, of course, he was her husband, because even now—as he walked backwards toward Mrs. Witherspoon's desk, naming a hundred different excuses and work concerns—Lord help her, she loved him.

Loved everything about him, for that matter.

Loved the mischievous lock of hair that fell on to his forehead at odd moments. Loved the clear green of his eyes and the curve of his lips, which were endearingly soft on an otherwise hard body. She loved the way she fit into him, her head nestling into the crook of his shoulder as they lay in bed. Loved the scent he left behind on the sheets. She had lain for several minutes upon waking this morning, holding his pillow to her.

Lingering in her feminine victory.

He had slept with her, stayed in her bed until dressing for the office. He had reassured her with his presence, because she had started to doubt herself. Not anymore. She was his wife; she must be his wife. He had made it so.

He backed up against Mrs. Witherspoon's desk and Susan stood before him, free hand on one hip, the other hand squeezing Baby Edward's wet fist.

"Susan, I mean, darling, I'm afraid I can't take today off, but I'll look at my calendar," he said. "In the meantime, how about if Mrs. Witherspoon looks after you today? She might even like the beach."

He took a long hard look at his secretary's empty desk. The phones were ringing, but he didn't seem to notice.

He glanced back at her, at the children.

And a look of despair passed across his face.

"Oh, no, Mrs. Witherspoon," he groaned. "What have you left me in charge of?"

Susan knew her husband was gracious in defeat and in victory. He knew when he was beaten. And he accepted it without complaint.

"The beach?" he asked, as if hearing her for the first time. "What a wonderful idea."

"And Mrs. Witherspoon?" Susan asked.

"She's…uh, taking a little personal time," Dean answered. "Maybe I should, too."

He distracted her with a clear, winning smile.

"We both need the time together," she said.

He picked up Baby Edward. Chelsea and Henry stared uncertainly.

"Come on, let's head for the beach," he said.

He led them back out through the hallway, stopping only long enough to tell the receptionist that he was taking the day off and that the Eastman negotiations needed to be rescheduled.

"But there's a reporter from the *Wall Street Journal* on the line," the receptionist cried. "He wants to know if you'll confirm or deny that your nanny…"

Dean led his family into the elevator.

"Just tell him I'm taking the wife and kids out for the day," he said as the doors slid shut behind them.

Chapter Ten

Considering that he was spending the day with a very delusional nanny, Dean Radcliffe was having fun.

Chicago's North Avenue beach was virtually empty on the weekday morning. The children were building a sand castle near the water's edge and Susan was languorously sunbathing beside him. A speedboat raced along the horizon and the waves rippled toward the shore.

He was having fun, but already becoming restless. Dean was a man of action, unused to leisure. Or maybe he found it hard to lay next to a beautiful woman in a bathing suit on the beach without wanting to reach out and...

He pulled his cell phone out of Susan's beach

bag. He started to dial just as Susan sat up and took the phone from him.

"What the...?"

She sprang to her feet, lightly stepped across the hot sand to the water's edge. Dean leapt after her just as she threw the phone across the water. The phone tripped across the surface twice and then kerplunk! It disappeared beneath the water's surface.

"Why'd you do that?" Dean demanded.

"You've made four phone calls in the past hour," Susan pointed out.

"I'm just checking in at the office," Dean protested. "I'm supposed to be handling a major merger today."

"You're supposed to be spending the day with your family, free of the cares of the business world," she corrected with mock severity. She wagged a finger in his face. "You should trust your employees do their jobs."

Dean stiffened.

"I can't. My most trusted employee Mrs. Witherspoon quit," he admitted.

"Why?"

"Because of the Eastman deal."

"Good for her," Susan quipped.

"How can you say that?"

"I wouldn't ordinarily tell you what to do with your business, but I think you're making a huge mistake taking apart that company and selling it.

You're hurting so many people, including yourself. And Mrs. Witherspoon is just reminding you of your foolishness.''

"It's not foolish, it's good business sense. And it will help a lot of people. The price I'll pay will make the Eastman family members comfortably wealthy for the rest of their lives. They'll never have to work again." His voice rose with his frustration that no one seemed to understand his vision. "The workers will get generous severance packages. The land will be put to good use. And Radcliffe Enterprises will make money. Everyone will benefit."

Susan looked over at the children building the sand castle.

"Not them."

He followed her gaze.

"What do they have to do with it?"

"Everything, Dean. Everything."

She took his hand and led him to the sand castle.

"Can we help, too?" she asked Chelsea.

Chelsea responded by shrieking as a wave lapped over the castle's edge. Henry shoveled furiously to stop the water's destructive force. Baby Edward started to cry.

"Here, let me," Dean said.

He knelt down in the cool, wet sand and pushed a wall of sand into place. With hours at their disposal, the family built a sturdy fortress to protect their castle. Their skin rubbed raw with sand, their faces ruddy with sun, they laughingly created a sanctuary that survived the gently rising tide.

"This is wonderful!" Chelsea cried out, as they put the last decorative pebbles on the sand tower's edges. "I can't remember the last time Daddy came with us."

"It was long before..." Henry began and he looked at Susan. "Before..."

"Before what?" Susan asked, puzzled.

Dean looked at his son, knowing Henry was thinking of the storm. The storm that had changed all their lives.

The children had put up a united front behind Susan, steadfastly refusing to acknowledge that she was not, in fact, their mother. He hadn't pressed the point, though he knew the issue would have to be faced soon. He hadn't wanted to upset the children.

Maybe, he thought as he surveyed the giant sand castle and his happy children, maybe he hadn't wanted to upset himself, either.

"It's been a long time," Dean said simply, rescuing Henry. But knowing he was avoiding the truth—that he hadn't spent much time at all with the children, had felt overwhelmed by their needs, since Nicole's death.

But, then, they hadn't spent much time together as a family before her death.

Chelsea smiled, and he knew his daughter well

enough to know that she was relieved that he hadn't made them remember that Susan was not really his wife, not really their mother.

Sometimes he found it hard to remember Susan was their nanny, he thought, as he watched her gather their towels, kiss a boo-boo on Baby Edward's knee and wrap her cover-up around her slim waist. The long shadows she cast on the white sand reminded him to check his watch.

Four-thirty.

Dean shook his wrist and checked again. He couldn't believe it. How had he managed to spend nearly eight hours on a beach with his family? Eight hours away from the office. And the world hadn't collapsed, at least as far as he knew.

He scrambled to his feet, grabbed Baby Edward from behind and hoisted him onto his shoulders.

"Come on. We should head home," he said.

"Home?" Susan asked, looking levelly at him. "Home or the office?"

Chelsea and Henry stared.

"Home," he said. Maybe Susan was right—if his employees couldn't run the office without him for one day, he hadn't hired the right employees.

He could only trust his judgment by trusting them.

He watched Susan flapping the towels, scattering sand to the wind.

She was a good wife—wise and caring, warm

and tolerant of his weaknesses, sexy as all get-out. A good wife, a good mother and a good lover, if her kisses were any indication.

What was he thinking of? he wondered as he turned away.

She's the nanny, he reminded himself, roughly shoving windswept hair back from his forehead.

"Now who's the one with delusions?" he asked aloud and was grateful that no one heard him.

They drove north on Sheridan Road, a picturesque path that followed the lake. They swept past the enchanted Tudors and cottages that once had been the summer homes and private getaways of Chicago's privileged class. When they reached Winnetka it was already six and the children complained of being hungry.

"Let's park here," Susan suggested as they turned the corner on Elm Street to a quaint block of shops and town houses.

Dean stopped in front of the Book Stall and Susan, borrowing his jacket for protection against the crisp night air, led them into the next-door toy shop. The children dispersed quickly in the dizzyingly arrayed displays of action figures, building sets and dolls.

Entwining her delicate fingers in his, Susan led him back to the counter where an elderly woman sat poised over her needlework.

"Hello, Susan," the woman said, looking up. "I hear you had quite an accident during the storm."

"Oh, I did," Susan agreed. "But I'm better now. A little bit of rest is all I needed. My husband took the day off to be with me and the kids. We thought we'd take a look around here for the children."

The shopkeeper peered at Dean from over her bifocals.

"Did you say husband?"

"Well, yes, Mrs. Cohen. You know Dean, don't you?"

"Congratulations, young man," Mrs. Cohen said. "And best wishes to you, my dear."

"Thank you," Susan replied, wondering if the toy store owner was losing her marbles.

"When did this happen?" Mrs. Cohen asked.

"When did what happen?"

"The wedding."

Now positive that Mrs. Cohen was having trouble with either her memory or her hearing or both, Susan didn't want to embarrass the toy shop owner.

Or herself. Because, come to think of it, she couldn't remember when she and Dean had wed. She glanced at Dean, wishing he would help her out. But he only regarded her thoughtfully.

"It happened a long time ago," Susan said vaguely.

Mrs. Cohen leaned forward and whispered conspiratorially.

"Was it a secret wedding?"

"Some secret wedding. Susan can tell you there was the usual white dress, flowers and tuxes," Dean said blandly. "She'll also tell you that we danced all night, and that was the best part of the wedding."

Susan smiled her gratitude.

"Mrs. Cohen, I really came in here to show Dean your Eastman bear display."

"Oh, Susan," the woman clucked. "You know there's a wait list for those bears."

"A wait list?" Dean asked.

"It's a mile long!" Mrs. Cohen barked, pulling a weathered notebook from a drawer beneath the counter. "Look at those names. If I put you down now, you might get a bear by Christmas."

"That's six months away!" Dean exclaimed. "But they're stockpiled with inventory at the factory. Can't you get a bear earlier than Christmas?"

"No, that's the best I can do." Mrs. Cohen shrugged. "They're very popular bears."

"So why aren't they in stock?" Dean asked.

"Trouble is, that company doesn't know how to get the bears to the stores."

"Who's their distributor?" Dean asked, and Susan caught the shift in tone that meant...business.

She drifted away to look at a display of play sets. Dean and Mrs. Cohen pored over the notebook of orders she had placed with Eastman. Susan smiled—her husband was doing what he did best.

Solving problems.

He was going to figure out a way for Eastman Bears to turn themselves around, even if he didn't know it.

She looked at toys while the children quietly placed their small selections on the counter beside Mrs. Cohen and Dean. She knew Dean would purchase them when he was done reviewing the paperwork that Mrs. Cohen had dragged out of the back room. The two of them were still talking heatedly about the good and bad points of the Eastman Bear Company when Susan and the children slipped out the door and went across the street to buy hot dogs and lemonade at the Depot Diner.

When the children were done with their dinner, Susan put them in the car. Baby Edward fell asleep before she buckled him in his car seat. When she went to retrieve her husband, Mrs. Cohen was putting the children's small toys in a shopping bag and Dean was bent over a notebook outlining the company's distributorship network.

"Come on, darling," Susan said, linking her arm in his. "Time for our dinner. Mrs. Cohen, I'm so sorry for my husband keeping you past your closing time."

"Oh, no problem." Mrs. Cohen shushed her. "If he ends up buying that company, there's a fair chance I'll get a few people off this waiting list. A lot of happy children could come of that."

"That would be wonderful!" Susan agreed, ignoring Dean's protest that he hadn't promised a single thing. "Good night, Mrs. Cohen."

"Good night, dear," Mrs. Cohen said. And then, as Dean opened the door for Susan, she added, "Susan, are you registered anywhere?"

"Registered?" Susan asked, puzzled.

"For wedding gifts."

"Oh, no, Mrs. Cohen, we're not," Susan said. She waved a cheery goodbye and whispered at Dean when they reached the car, "I think she's a little confused. Imagine sending a wedding present to a couple who've been married as long as we have!"

"I don't think she's confused at all," Dean said, glancing back at the shop. "I think she's one of the smartest businesspersons I've met in a long time. Now, shall we go home?"

They drove down the quiet, dark streets until they reached the winding path to the Radcliffe house. Dean carried a sleeping Henry up to bed, while Susan carried Baby Edward up to his. Chelsea followed groggily and didn't protest when she was put to bed immediately after brushing her teeth.

Susan went upstairs to take a quick shower and change into a comfortable pair of jeans and a

T-shirt. As she was drying her hair with a towel, she wandered into Dean's study.

"Darling, what do you want for dinner?" she asked, and then gasped as she saw the pained expression on his face. "Dean, what is it?"

Dean's eyes were as cloudy as a storm-ridden sea, and she felt the first startling tremors of fear.

Chapter Eleven

Dean abruptly punched the erase button on the answering machine. The rewinding tape shrieked like a singer on helium.

"Nothing's wrong," he said abruptly.

And he moved quickly to distract her, because he knew that she was smart enough to read his expression better than anyone else he had ever known. She would know he wasn't happy.

Hell, he was worried sick.

And all because he had gotten exactly what he had demanded—information on Susan's family. The investigator said he had everything. The truth was just a phone call away.

Now Dean wasn't sure he wanted to know.

He put his arms around her and kissed her lightly

on the cheek, careful to not overstep his own boundaries of honor but allowing himself the bittersweet pleasure of her soft flesh against his lips. And trying his best to smile through it all.

"Darling, you look worried," Susan said, concern lining her forehead.

"It's nothing," he said, smoothing away those tiny lines. "How 'bout some dinner?"

"Are you sure there's nothing going on? Nothing I should know about?"

"Absolutely. It's just…just business. Nothing I can't handle. Put it out of your mind—I don't want to let go of the magic of our day together. Remember, you were the one who wanted me to take a day off. You haven't yet gotten your twenty-four hours' worth."

She brightened.

"Fair enough," she said. "Would you like to eat out on the courtyard tonight?"

"Sure. After a shower I'll join you," he said, and as her footsteps receded from the study, he closed his eyes and gave up trying to stifle his unease.

The private detective hired by the head of security for Radcliffe Enterprises. He claimed he had found the information Dean was looking for. Dean should call back. Now. Tonight. The detective would take his call no matter the hour.

But Dean couldn't. He knew that phone call

would mean the end of being with Susan. Her family, whoever they might be, would come for her. She would remember who she was. She would be embarrassed and he would be…emotionless, because he dealt with grief by losing touch with his own heart.

She had opened up something inside of him, but it was something that would close back up as soon as she left him.

And she would leave him.

Just as Nicole had.

He looked out the study window to the courtyard. Susan was throwing a white lace tablecloth on the wrought-iron table and had lit votive candles around the courtyard. He could hear her humming a tune—she belonged here, he thought defiantly.

No, she didn't.

She had a family out there, ready to bring Susan to her senses. She deserved to know them. Now.

He should go downstairs right now and tell her—but he couldn't.

He didn't know if it was because he was selfish or if it was because he loved her.

And couldn't believe that she wouldn't go. Go without looking back. Leaving him behind. Alone.

In the kitchen, Susan poured two glasses of white wine and put them on a black lacquer tray next to a plate of delicate phyllo-wrapped appetizers. She hummed a jazzy tune as she carried the tray out the pantry door to the courtyard. It was a cool, crisp summer evening—the kind she liked—with the promise of an impromptu dinner party for two.

The kind she liked.

As she put the tray down on the table, Dean walked up behind her, wrapping her shoulders in a pink sweater she recognized from her closet.

"Chilly?" he asked.

She turned around, a captive in rock-hard muscle and soft, fluffy cashmere.

"I'm never chilly as long as I have you to keep me warm," she replied huskily.

He was startled by her boldness, but she shushed him with a full, knowing kiss. At first he held back, his mouth tight and closed. But she was his wife— she knew him, knew his need for pleasure, knew the way he liked it. Hot and deep. She teased and taunted the flesh of his lower lip with her mouth until at last he relented. She slid her tongue between his lips and touched the rough tip of his own.

That touch set off an explosion of feeling. He took over, kissing her with an ardor that commanded hers—leaving her shaken and breathless. A little shivery. But still, she flattened her aching breasts against his chest and let her hands travel down his back....

Thank goodness they were married, or she'd never act in this wanton way!

"Let's go inside," she whispered. "We can have dinner later."

Her invitation left no room for doubt about her intentions.

"Susan, I want to. But..."

"Then let's go upstairs."

"I can't."

"Dean, the children are asleep."

"That's not the problem."

He relinquished her and reached for a wineglass for her.

She took it but did not drink. She already felt tipsy enough. But not so out of her mind that she didn't see his agitation.

She thought back to the moment she had stepped into the study.

"Dean, what was that phone message about?" she asked. "When you were in the study, you were listening to the phone messages and you looked so worried. Is something going on at the office that you need to take care of?"

"It's nothing," he said curtly, picking up his own glass and sitting down at the table.

"Nothing?"

"Nothing at the office," he added significantly.

"Dean, I know you. There's something wrong. Something very wrong. Whatever it is...we can face it. Together."

He took a deep breath.

"Susan, what if you weren't my wife?"

Susan indignantly turned away.

"It's that nanny thing again, isn't it?"

"Yes. But just for a moment, pretend I'm right."

Susan shook her head.

"Susan, please."

"All right, let's pretend I'm really the children's nanny," she said, barely suppressing her irritation. He was ruining a beautiful evening. But she loved him, and so, with the weary voice of love tested once too often, she added, "And if I am the children's nanny, why can't you still make love to me? Lots of men have staged seductions like that. I can pretend to be an innocent, you can pretend you're doing something very naughty."

"I can't take advantage of you," he said stiffly.

"Spare me. I can take care of myself."

"You can when you're Mrs. Radcliffe, but when you're Susan the nanny... Besides, I had a wife."

Susan gasped. This had gone too far!

"Her name was Nicole," Dean continued. "She was beautiful and perfect in every way. It's just she didn't love me. And I didn't love her."

"Why did you marry her?" Susan asked.

"Because I wanted to prove I was a steady, reliable man," Dean said. "I was a wild young stud. I had had a few women—maybe more than a man should. I had a reputation as a playboy. A playboy with a golden touch at business. It was time for me to prove myself in another way. I wanted to prove I could head a family as well as a corporation.''

''And then what happened to this perfect wife?''

Dean looked away, but before his face was lost to shadow, Susan saw the very real pain he was going through.

She reached out to take his hand in hers, reassuring him. At first he recoiled, and then, as if sensing that she loved him, loved him even when she didn't believe him, he took her hand into his own firm grasp.

''She wasn't so perfect,'' he admitted reluctantly. ''Although not many people knew that. She led two lives. There was a split between the woman she wanted to be and the woman the world wanted her to be. She wanted to drink and party and...meet other men. So she did. And then one night we had an argument—another argument. I wanted her to spend more time with the children and less with the groundskeeper she had hired.''

''So what happened?''

''She was drinking. I went back to the office. The children were at home. She drove away. She ran into the brick wall out there at the end of the path. Her car went into the ravine. She died instantly.''

''You must have felt terrible.''

''I felt I had killed her. Because I didn't let her be who she wanted to be. Someone else.''

"But she could have asked you for a divorce if that's how she felt."

"She didn't want that," he said with a bitter laugh. "With the Radcliffe name and money she was welcome everywhere. Everywhere she wanted to go."

"What about the children?"

"The children miss her but don't remember much about her. Don't remember her because she didn't have a lot to do with them. Nicole felt she had given me more than my due. She gave me three children to carry on the Radcliffe name."

"And when did I show up?" Susan asked. "If, indeed, I'm not your wife."

"I hired you after I lost every other nanny and housekeeper the agency sent me," he said. "I'm very hard on people. I have very high expectations."

"No!" Susan cried out sarcastically. "Dean Radcliffe hard on people? I never would have guessed."

"You're teasing me."

"Yes, I am. You deserve to be teased. We make a great pair. You think I'm deluding myself that I'm your wife. And I'm deluding myself thinking that you've got a warm and giving heart buried beneath that rock-hard chest. Two of a kind, aren't we?"

He smiled, but the mirth died quickly, replaced

by something more base, something more animal, something that as a gentleman he knew he had to fight. He wanted her, needed her, ached for her, his body strained against chains of his own making.

"Oh, Susan, I want to carry you upstairs to that bedroom and make you mine, but I can't because tomorrow morning you might wake up to the truth that you're not my wife. And you'd hate me for taking advantage of you."

"Maybe I wouldn't hate you," she answered, knowing that her physical desire for him was so sharp and so demanding that she wasn't thinking clearly.

This man was linked to her so powerfully that even if her world came crashing down around her— and their marriage with it—she'd still find no other place that would thrill her as much as in his arms.

Still, she knew that her sense of right and wrong hadn't changed—whether she was a wife or a nanny.

"I don't know if I'd feel right making love to you if I weren't your wife, but, Dean, is that the only reason you won't make love to me?"

"Yes," he said without hesitation.

She leaned forward to kiss him.

"But, Susan, I won't take advantage of you," he warned.

"Then let me take just a little bit of advantage of you," she said. And she kissed him not on the lips as she knew he expected, but on the cheek. Lightly.

Just a little bit of advantage.

"I've got to check on the swordfish," she said throatily. "I'm sure it's burnt to a crisp now."

They had both forgotten how hungry they were, or maybe the teasing sexual desire had heightened their body's every need. They ate the swordfish, which hadn't burnt, with rice and grilled vegetables. They talked of everything—the children, the neighborhood, politics, recent movies—everything except the urgent questions between them.

Would you still love me if you weren't my husband?

Would you think I've taken advantage of you if you weren't my wife?

As they finished their key lime pie, Susan felt the rigors of the day catch up with her. Dr. Sugar had told her to stay in bed for at least a week and here she was—having returned from a long day at the beach with the children.

She looked across the table to Dean.

She wouldn't have traded this day for the world.

I wish all this were mine, she thought wistfully.

And suddenly she felt her heart pounding with terror. She gulped and hid her trembling lips behind her napkin, though Dean didn't seem to notice her sudden change of mood.

I wish all this were mine.

The words coursed through her blood, pulsating like a unrepentant drum. Memories came back, and as she lifted her hand to take a cooling sip of wine, she noticed the twinkling bracelet on her hand.

With three silver charms. One for Henry. One for Chelsea. One for Baby Edward.

She remembered him giving the bracelet to her.

Mrs. Witherspoon must have picked it out.

Dear, efficient Mrs. Witherspoon.

Images and words and sensations swirled like a kaleidoscope, and then fell into place.

She knew exactly who she was.

Who she had been.

Susan Graves.

And what a fool she was making of herself.

She got to her feet and Dean looked at her, startled.

"Are you all right?" he asked.

She nodded first, and then shook her head.

She wasn't all right.

She wasn't all right at all.

She wasn't Susan Radcliffe. And he wasn't her husband. And this wasn't her house. And those weren't her children upstairs.

She was the nanny. Susan Graves. The nanny who had first stepped inside the house a year ago. Scrawny, insecure, aching for a home, with a ratty old suitcase that had been her only home for so many years.

She wasn't part of the family at all.

She had simply wanted so much, wanted so much to be part of this family, to be part of his life, that when the lightning had coursed up Wiley's chain from the gardener's shed to her wet hand, her brain had snapped, shifted its reality, from what was true to what she wished for.

"Darling?" he asked.

She knew he would give her proof tomorrow. Or even if he didn't, she knew she wouldn't be able to stand the unbearable shame another day. The shame of having acted so crazy, of having had such delusions, of having thrown herself at him, practically begging him to make love to her. Of having danced and laughed and called this home, this man, her own. And he had been so patient.

So utterly patient.

She wouldn't be able to bear it.

Tomorrow.

But she had tonight.

Because she remembered her birthday wish, made but a scant few days ago.

She wanted all this to be hers.

Just for a little while.

Just to be his for a little while.

Tomorrow morning was soon enough.

"I'm really very tired," she said, hoping that her trembling wasn't too apparent.

"I'll carry you up to bed," he said.

She should have refused him, but she didn't. She wanted to be his wife just a moment longer. He picked her up and carried her through the patio doors, across the long living room and up the stairs to the master bedroom. He laid her upon the bed as gently as a delicate flower, eased her sneakers from her feet and pulled the coverlet over her.

"Will you come to bed?" she asked, and added, "darling?"

He groaned, and she thought he would refuse. His jaw rippled with tension. And then he smiled tightly and she wondered if he knew that she knew exactly who she was.

"Of course," he said.

And she closed her eyes, smiling bravely against the knowledge that tomorrow was coming.

Smiling bravely because just for tonight she was his.

Tomorrow, Susan Radcliffe would disappear and Susan Graves would take her place.

Chapter Twelve

Susan groggily opened her eyes and watched Dean's reflection in the gold-filigreed mirror as he finished the precise folds of his tie. He smiled as his bright, true eyes noticed hers.

"Morning, beautiful," he said. He frowned. "Does your head hurt again?"

"No, no, it's not that," Susan said quickly. "I'm fine."

Striding across the bedroom, he leaned down to kiss her hair and murmured that he'd be at the office. Susan felt an ache in her head, in her chest, in her whole body, an ache of remembrance, an ache of missing him. Already, though he wasn't even gone.

This kiss, chaste and fleeting, was to be their last.

Beneath the coverlet, she balled her fingers up so that her nails stabbed her palms. She would not, she would not beg him to stay.

"Be home at five," he whispered.

"I'll have dinner ready," she said, though she knew that those wifely words were false.

He flung his suit jacket over his shoulder and strode out the door, taking his scent with him. For a brief moment, he hesitated in the hallway. She knew he had sensed…something. But then he left, taking the steps two at a time, whistling a jazzy tune.

She rolled over on the bed and felt his space. Where he had lain, chastely holding her, all through the wordless night.

He hadn't made love to her, she knew, because he was an honorable man. Or maybe just because she wasn't his kind of woman.

Because she wasn't the confident, womanly Susan Radcliffe. Susan Radcliffe had style, could make a dinner party for two or twenty, could dance without stepping on her partner's toes, and she kissed like a woman who could pleasure her husband.

Susan Graves was another woman, a woman decidedly less sure of herself. A woman who faded into the background. A woman who smelled of cooking and cleaning. A woman with her own restrictive rules—and one of those rules was to not make love to a man who wasn't her husband. But a man as strongly sensual and as worldly as Dean needed Susan Radcliffe—not Susan Graves.

She had wanted him, surprising herself at the quick, instinctive sexual response to him. To the press of his flesh as he slept at her side. To the sleek definition of his muscles as he gripped her while he thought she slept. She had felt the heat spreading from her stomach and down through her legs. She knew that if she ever were his wife, their lovemaking would be white-hot combustible—and it filled her with longing.

Susan Radcliffe was no frigid, shrinking violet. She could be uninhibited and wanton. She could be as eager for sex as Dean was. She could learn all the ways a woman makes a man feel like a man.

But she wasn't his wife.

She was the nanny.

And he had humored her delusion as only the finest gentleman could, but in the end, she had to concede the awful truth.

He had done so because he pitied her.

She had grown up with pity. First, when her parents had died. Then, in the succession of foster homes and placements. Pity was one thing she hated, and the one thing Dean offered.

And so she had nothing to take with her but memories of nearly complete happiness. And the knowledge that within her very proper and determinedly sensible exterior there lurked a sexual fireball.

A sexual fireball that would never spark, because there would never be a Dean Radcliffe to set her body ablaze.

And she had her pride—she would never take his pity again.

Reluctantly pushing aside the embroidered sheets, she padded up to her third-floor room. She packed quickly and efficiently, for there wasn't much that she, as Susan Graves, carried with her. A few clothes, a photo album that she couldn't bear to open and a dozen pictures the children had made her.

She looked at the bracelet, twinkling with three charms. She wouldn't give it back—it had been a birthday present, after all.

It would remain a bittersweet reminder of Henry, Chelsea, Baby Edward—and Dean.

She walked down to the first floor, leaving her suitcase in the front foyer. Then she went into the kitchen, fixing waffles—the children loved waffles—as a special treat.

The children came down in their nightclothes, drawn by the vanilla and maple syrup smells.

"Waffles?" Chelsea asked. "But it's not Sunday and it's nobody's birthday."

"Don't remind her," Henry counseled wisely.

"She might make us eat cereal. I love waffles more."

They all agreed they loved waffles and Susan asked the children to help set the table. While they ate their first forkfuls, she slipped out to the study and called Mrs. Witherspoon at home.

"I'm not working for him any longer," Mrs. Witherspoon said flatly. "Not after what he's threatening to do at Eastman Bear Company."

"He won't break apart the company," Susan said, surprising herself with the prediction.

"But there's a meeting scheduled with Mr. Eastman later this morning."

"He won't take it apart."

"You're sure?"

"As only a wife can be."

"But you're not his wife," Mrs. Witherspoon pointed out.

"I was for a few days. Long enough to know. Please, Mrs. Witherspoon, the children need you. And Dean needs you, if he'd just admit it."

Mrs. Witherspoon came to the house as Henry and Chelsea were finishing putting away the dishes.

"Give me a big hug, Chelsea," Susan said, trying desperately to keep her voice from betraying her emotions. "I've got to go out...go out for a while."

The three children crowded around her and she

crouched down and kissed each one in turn and received their tight hugs. She memorized the feel of their bodies, the talc and syrup smell of them and the little words of love they said so quickly and offhandedly because they couldn't know this was goodbye forever.

And then she got up, avoiding Mrs. Witherspoon's eyes, and picked up her suitcase.

"You really feel you have to leave?" Mrs. Witherspoon asked.

"Yes, and please don't tell him I'm gone until he comes home tonight," Susan said.

She knew he'd feel obligated to try to find her, and she wanted to get a head start on him.

Enough to outrun him.

Enough to escape his terrible pity.

"Want me to call you a cab?"

"No, thanks," Susan replied. "I'll leave the way I came."

She walked out the front door and down the path. The sun was clear, the birds were singing, the trees were lush and green—but Susan felt nothing but cold and emptiness inside her.

She had almost reached the road when she heard Chelsea.

"Wait! Wait!" the child cried, her legs pumping furiously as she ran down the path to Susan.

Susan put down her suitcase and caught Chelsea in her arms.

"Are you leaving for good?" Chelsea demanded.
Susan sighed.

"Yes, Chelsea, I have to go."

"Does that mean you're not going to be our mom anymore?"

Susan closed her eyes, realizing how terribly her amnesia had affected the children. How terribly unfair to the children this incident had been.

And she had never, never wanted to hurt the children.

"You have a mother," she said cautiously. "She's in heaven and watches over you. And you'll have a new nanny. She'll be wonderful. And you have a…a daddy. And he loves you."

"But I want you."

"No, Chelsea, you'll always have a memory of me. But I have to go."

Chelsea's face went ash white and then suddenly red, bright red. She burst into tears, angrily struggled out of Susan's arms and raced away toward the house.

"Go ahead and leave us!" she screamed. "Go on! Leave! We don't care anyhow!"

And she turned and marched back up the path. Henry and Baby Edward had come out onto the front porch. They stared silently.

As she reached the porch, Chelsea kicked a rock into the grass.

"Chelsea, darling..." Susan pleaded and then the words died on her lips.

She had to let her go.

She had to let all of them go.

But she understood the anger and the betrayal and the fear and the pain. She had felt all those things herself, long ago, when she was not much older than Chelsea.

Maybe, she thought as she turned away from the house, maybe that's why she had wished so much to be part of the Radcliffe world, why the lightning had affected her so. Because she wanted so badly to have a family, because there was such a deep need inside of her.

A need she never expressed. Not even to herself.

Of course, love was another explanation.

Because she loved Dean Radcliffe.

And had had no idea how to tell him that she loved him and no hope that he would love a woman as simple and uncomplicated as Susan Graves.

She felt a sudden dizziness as she stepped out onto the road to town. She remembered Dr. Sugar's admonition to take it easy, but she knew she didn't have a choice. She had to get to the bus stop.

She quickened her pace.

She would get out of Winnetka.

Before anyone, out of pity, asked her to stay.

She forced one foot in front of the other.

"The subject, Susan Graves, was orphaned at the age of eight," the private investigator read dryly from his notes. "She was sent first to a privately run foster home, but when budget cuts hit the social service agency a year later, the foster home was shut down. She was then sent to a state-run orphanage, until the age of eleven, when a private placement was located for her. Though she was not in any way a behavioral problem, the private placement only lasted for two years...."

"Enough," Dean said, putting his hands on his head. He looked at the two men sitting in front of him. Clearly in awe of his office, the head of security and his hand-picked investigator shifted in their seats. "Does she have any family left?"

"No," the investigator said, and he flipped through his yellow legal pad. "There was a second cousin of the mother, but she died in 1990."

"And she's never married?"

The two employees exchanged glances.

"No, never married. No children. A boyfriend in high school, but..."

"But what?" Dean pounced. Somehow he needed to know this part of her life, though it had no bearing on finding Susan a home.

"The boyfriend was apparently nothing serious." The investigator shrugged. "And he married another woman a year after graduation."

Dean leaned back in his chair and stared out at the fog rolling in from the lake.

"I can understand why she would develop this delusion," the investigator supplied tentatively. "And I understand how you'd like to have this matter resolved as quickly as possible."

"Actually, you wouldn't understand at all," Dean said under his breath.

His new secretary, a robust blonde named Becky who did her nails at her desk, walked into the office.

"It's your daughter on line two," she said.

Dean picked up the receiver.

It could only mean trouble.

"Yes, Chelsea?" he asked, fighting back his dread.

"We want her back," Chelsea said, gulping once.

Dean knew she had been crying. He could hear Baby Edward howling in the background.

"Want who back?" Although he already knew. And despaired.

"Susan. She's packed her suitcase and left us."

Dean swallowed. Hard. He was used to holding on to his emotions, but the news Chelsea delivered nearly made him cry out with frustration and despair.

"I'm coming home, Chelsea," he said.

"Bring her back."

"I will," he promised his children.

He hung up and put on his jacket.

He ignored Becky's outstretched hand with "just a few letters" that needed to be signed. He barely managed a goodbye to the head of security and his investigator.

He strode out of the office, taking the stairs instead of the elevator because he figured that he could beat it down to ground level.

But it wasn't until he was on I-94 heading back to Winnetka that he realized that Chelsea had called her Susan. The children weren't calling her mom.

That meant the wonderful and tender and delicate charade was over.

It meant that Susan knew exactly who she was. And who she wasn't.

"I've come to see my wife," Dean said at the fourth-floor nurse's station. Dean raked a hand through his hair. After hours of fruitless searching, he'd gotten a call from the hospital telling him Susan had been admitted after collapsing on the road. His relief had combined with a palpable fear and he'd raced to the hospital like a man possessed.

Dr. Sugar, sitting there and reviewing a patient's chart, looked up.

"Oh, really?"

Dean ground his teeth.

"Yes, really. My wife. Where is she?"

"I thought the last time you were here you said—"

"I know what I said. Just let me see her."

"She's resting now."

"I've got to see her."

Dr. Sugar closed his chart and stared implacably at Dean.

"She pushed herself too hard. What she was doing on a hot, humid summer day carrying a suitcase down Willow Road remains a mystery to me. She was supposed to be resting."

"Is she going to be all right?"

"Tough to say. She collapsed from dehydration and exhaustion. She needs rest and she needs fluids. She needs a little peace and quiet," the doctor added pointedly. "The same prescription I gave her when I released her into your care just a few days ago."

"She'll have all those things if she comes back home with me."

Dr. Sugar shook his head.

"She knows exactly who she is now," he said. "And she's not reentering your house as the very delusional and very pitied nanny."

"She wouldn't have to do that. She could come home as my wife."

Both men were stunned by Dean's words. They stared at each other for several moments, Dean defiantly certain and Dr. Sugar openmouthed.

At last the doctor stood up.

"Come with me," he said. "But I warn you. Don't say anything you don't mean. And don't mean anything you don't say."

Chapter Thirteen

In the bathroom attached to her hospital room, Susan clutched the sides of the sink and stared dismally into the mirror. The fluorescent light was harsh and unforgiving.

Her faded hospital gown, tied at the back, was pea green and ugly. Her lips were palest, parched pink, without the cranberry-colored lipstick that had made Susan Radcliffe look so sassy. And her hair was pulled back in a long tight braid—very sensible, but very boring. Not the way Susan Radcliffe would wear hers.

Susan heard the outer door open and assumed another nurse had come to check on her. She didn't remember everything—but what she did remember made her cringe. She had left the Radcliffe estate, had walked six miles to the nearest bus stop and then a combination of weariness, sorrow and hunger had taken over. She had fainted, awakening in the emergency room to Dr. Sugar's annoyingly insistent "tsk, tsk, tsk."

He thought overdoing it was what had made her faint. Susan knew better—it was sheer despair that had short-circuited her brain and her body.

She threw cold water on her face to soothe her skin that had been made raw with the salty tears that wouldn't stop coming.

She cautiously walked back into the hospital room, ready for whatever poking, prodding, medicating or blood-pressure taking the nurse had in mind for her.

"Susan," Dean said, his voice every bit as caressing as if she were still...his wife.

Her heartbeat could have shorted out the EKG machine.

Dean stood by the bed with a paper-wrapped bouquet of flowers in his hands. His white shirt was utterly businesslike and proper—but without a tie and suit coat, with the top button undone and the cuffs pulled back, he looked like a rogue, a beefcake pin-up, a heartthrob, a gambler.

Some justice in this world! He looked great, and she looked...like plain, ordinary sensible Susan Graves.

She wanted to run, her eyes reflexively darting

around to find an escape route. There was none—
he was simply too big, too commanding of a man
to evade. Cornered, she felt like fighting—pushing
him away, demanding that he leave. But the fight
had been worn out of her, and all she had left was
embarrassment.

This was the man for whom she had harbored a
secret and all-encompassing crush—and lightning
had released her innermost passions for him, her
innermost fantasies of being his wife, of being the
mother of his children, of being his lover.

And she had acted on every one of those, except
of course, for the ultimate fantasy that he, as a gentleman, had declined to make a reality.

Or maybe being a gentleman had nothing to do
with it.

His tastes don't run to my kind, she thought, remembering the pictures of Nicole before he'd
packed them away several months ago. His wife
had been glamorous and polished, sophisticated and
model-perfect.

It was humiliating to stand before the man she
loved—yes, *loved,* and know that he had pitied her,
had humored her delusions and had waited patiently
for her to come to her senses.

She felt a hot, furious blush cover her chest and
her face. She could imagine what she looked like.
She wasn't the type for dainty, shell pink blushes.

No, she was the kind of woman who burst into splotchy scarlet.

She wished he'd leave.

Hand her the flowers that Mrs. Witherspoon must have foisted on him.

Say his goodbyes.

Get it over with.

Stop being such a gentleman, because being a gentleman only made it worse for her.

If he acted like a jerk now, she could salvage something of her pride.

"What are you doing here?" she asked with as much dignity as she could muster, and sat down on the bed.

"I've come to take you home," he said.

"Oh, no, you don't," she said, warring with herself.

It would be so easy to give in.

"Susan, come on home. The children are desperate for you. And, while I thank you for somehow persuading Mrs. Witherspoon to come back, she hasn't gotten the hang of making peanut-butter sandwiches and can't find Chelsea's favorite jeans."

Susan shook her head. "You're being very nice."

"Very few people have ever accused me of that."

She turned her face against his winning smile.

"You're being nice," Susan repeated, keeping her voice as steady as possible. "And I want you to go home. And let me go on with my life."

He sat on the edge of the bed. She leaned back, back out of the reach of his scent and his charm.

"Listen, Susan, I'm a proud man, a hard man, a man who doesn't like to beg. I haven't had much practice at talking to a woman who doesn't want to talk to me—so I might be clumsy with this. But I'll play it completely straight. Susan, I want you to come home with me."

She shook her head.

"I'd really like to but I'm too much like you to say yes," she said. "Oh, don't look so startled. I'm not the head of a company and I don't drive a Porsche—but I'm proud and I'm tough and I want to hold my head up high. Just like you. I can't go back to your house—even though I miss...I miss the children very much. I can't go back because I've made a complete and utter fool of myself. Think about it, Dean. In my shoes, would you come back?"

"It can be just like it was before," he said, ignoring her question. Because they both knew the answer. He wouldn't come back. She wouldn't, either.

"No, it can't be the same," Susan corrected gently. "We can't forget. Either one of us."

"Then it can be better," he said urgently. "Susan, we learned this week. We learned how much..."

"How much what?"

"How much we love each other."

She stared at him, wanting so much to believe him. Wanting so much to simply say "Yes" to him. Wanting him so much that she would accept anything—any arrangement where she could stay.

But she couldn't. She had revealed everything about the depth of her feeling for him—he must regard her as some kind of innocent child with a puppylike crush on him. Maybe it built up his ego. Maybe he felt it his due—having grown up with women chasing him, and the Radcliffe fortune— with great enthusiasm. Maybe it made him feel responsible for her—oh, how she hated that.

More likely, he simply felt nothing.

Nothing but pity.

"How much we love each other?" she repeated hollowly.

"Enough to ask you to come and be with me," he said. "Me and my children."

"What as?"

"What do you mean, what as?"

"As your nanny? As your housekeeper? As your secret mistress?"

Susan saw him flinch at her words, strongly said, but strongly felt. She had to make him understand why she couldn't return to his household. She had been at his table, in his bed as his wife. She couldn't be anything less....

He lifted his chin, having made his decision.

"As my wife," he said.

Susan gasped and let herself lean back into the pillows.

His wife?

Oh, how she had fantasized, how she had dreamt, how she had longed for this.

But not for it to be this way.

"Why do you want to marry me?"

"Because I love you."

His words, simply issued and a reminder of what they had shared, should have been enough. And yet, for Susan, they weren't. The words were simply a new challenge.

Because she had heard those words before, and the promise carried within each syllable had been broken. Too many times. By her parents who, tragically, had died so young. By her foster parents, whose hearts were large enough but whose wallets were too small for an extra child at their table. By workers at the orphanage.

Susan was realistic about the word *love*. She knew that Dean was a strong, proud, vibrant man who could love only a very special woman.

She wasn't sure she was that woman.

But she was certain he didn't know, either.

"Why? Why do you love me?"

"Why does any man love a woman?" he defended.

"Just tell me why."

"Because you're fun and you're sexy and you're confident and smart and you smell good. Oh, and you look much better than Wiley in a dress."

"That's your wife you're talking about."

"Nicole?" he asked, eyes narrowing.

"No, your wife. Susan Radcliffe. The woman I was before I remembered who I am."

"But that's you."

"No, it isn't me. I was Susan Radcliffe because lightning rearranged my brain. I was a different woman for a week. That's the woman you fell in love with. You lived with Susan Graves for nearly a year and didn't notice she existed."

"Lightning didn't give you any new qualities that weren't there already."

Susan shook her head. How would he ever understand? She wasn't Susan Radcliffe—a confident, sexy, sassy woman with pizzazz. She was Susan Graves—a serious, shy woman who was good with kids.

Who smelled not of designer perfume, but of vanilla and cake.

"Please marry me, Susan," Dean said, leaning forward to kiss her. "Come home. Come home to all of us."

She wanted to turn away, wanted to hang on to

the last vestiges of pride. She had made a fool of herself, flinging herself at Dean.

She had kissed him, danced with him, tried to lure him into bed. And he had suffered all this with as much good humor as he could have.

He had even developed his own delusion that he loved her.

When all there really must be was pity.

Oh, how she hated pity.

She wanted to turn away, and yet she couldn't. She loved him with every fiber of her being, wanted every last kiss he had to offer. Every last kiss that she would treasure to the end of her days. More precious than diamonds.

She parted her lips. He touched her mouth with his, softly, so softly.

And in that moment, she thought she could feel his love for her.

His tongue darted into her mouth, pleasuring the tender flesh within. She felt the first trembling of tears, tears at the joy and wonder of it.

But the moment couldn't last. She wasn't his wife. He loved a woman who didn't exist.

Their kiss was everything—and yet it was not enough.

She pushed him away, and he looked as if he would protest, but a nurse came in, efficient and with no interest in negotiating. Visiting hours were over. Now.

"Tomorrow," Dean said, kissing her once more, but lightly. "We'll talk about this tomorrow. And I want you to know that I'm very persuasive."

She nodded silently, but didn't promise anything she couldn't give him.

Dean came home to find Mrs. Witherspoon and Wiley asleep in front of the television in the children's rec room. He flipped off the TV, leaned down to help slip Mrs. Witherspoon's feet out of her sensible pumps and pulled an afghan over her stockinged legs.

Wiley never stopped snoring.

"Some watch dog you are," Dean said, leaning over to scratch Wiley's ears.

Then he went upstairs. In Chelsea's room, the children had built a tent of blankets and pushed together chairs. They were asleep, Henry with his arms around a teddy bear—an Eastman bear, Dean noted. Chelsea had one arm around Baby Edward and the other clutched her Barbie.

They looked so peaceful.

He realized he really was a lucky man to have children who had survived the death of their mother with as much strength as they had shown.

Then he noticed Henry's eyes twitching, squinting really.

"All right, kids, you're up past your bedtime," Dean said.

The kids opened their eyes.

"We thought you'd be mad if we weren't already asleep," Henry said.

"No, I'm not angry," Dean said, surprising himself. He was ordinarily quite disciplined about the kids' schedules. He crouched down to their tent. "Can I come in?"

"Sure," Chelsea invited. "But where's Susan?"

The three children waited anxiously while he thought about what to tell them. As he looked at each of them in turn, he realized how out of touch he had become.

Chelsea was growing. She had teeth missing, and new ones coming in.

Baby Edward's face was getting thinner, a good thing since he had looked like the Pillsbury Doughboy when he was a baby.

And Henry looked so much more serious, as if he were already aping his father's take on the world.

Dean knew who had made it possible for him to look at his children again—to see them and not be thrown back into the vortex of terrible memories.

Susan. Susan had brought him back—with love. Her love that was so boundless and selfless.

He needed her.

He had to make her his wife.

Tomorrow. It would happen tomorrow.

"What would you think of Susan and me... together?" he asked.

"You mean, I'm supposed to think about the two of you at the same exact time?" Henry asked.

"No, silly, he's telling us that him and Susan are going to get married for real," Chelsea corrected.

All three smiled at their dad.

"Really?" Baby Edward asked.

"I think she'll say yes," Dean said. "I might have to do some persuading, but I'm pretty good at it."

"She'll be our mom?" Henry asked.

And then Chelsea grew somber.

"What's the matter?" Dean asked softly.

"I was wondering about Mom, our real mom."

Dean took a deep breath.

"Let's talk about Mom," he said.

He knew that this was only the first of many times that he'd have to talk about Nicole with the children. There'd be other conversations, many conversations, many questions, and he'd have to give answers that were right for every age.

But this was the first time. The first time he hadn't simply closed his eyes and turned away at the mention of his late wife.

He looked at each child in turn. He began to talk and he also began to listen.

Chapter Fourteen

Make a wish, Susan thought as she stared at the moss-covered fountain in front of the hospital's main entrance. She threw several pennies—they kerplunked and disappeared into the water.

Making a wish is exactly what got me into this mess, she thought ruefully.

But she made a final wish anyway—that Chelsea, Henry and Baby Edward would one day understand why she had to leave them.

She reached into the bottom of her bag and threw in a last copper coin. For Dean. He would understand, wouldn't he?

"Where to, lady?" the cabbie asked, hoisting her ragged suitcase into the trunk and slamming the lid.

"The bus station," Susan replied as she slipped into the back seat.

The cab eased away from the curb and glided down Elm Street. Her heart galloped as she realized they were heading toward the Radcliffe house, but then she relaxed as she figured out the driver was simply taking a shortcut to the station. She peered down the long, winding path leading toward the house, which was itself invisible from the street.

I got my wish, she thought. This was mine, just for a while. And who could ask for more than that?

It wasn't the fine house or the land or the fancy clothes or the champagne that she had been granted—although each was nice in its own way. No, it was the children and the love and the belonging and, especially, the man.

She loved Dean Radcliffe and it wasn't just a crush or a schoolgirl infatuation—it was a love that was deep and enduring. Maybe she'd marry someday, but she knew she'd never find a man who could measure up to the standard Dean created. Dean Radcliffe would be a shadow that she couldn't shake, the man that she would carry in her heart. For always.

Still, she had gotten more than she was entitled to—her birthday wish had been fulfilled if only for a little while. And now it was time for her to move on—the charade couldn't last. The enchantment could only end with disillusionment as Dean discovered that she wasn't like the glamorous and sassy Susan Radcliffe.

From now on, Susan intended on living her life firmly grounded in reality, not fantasy. No more daydreaming. No more storybook tales with happy endings. Maybe Dean had been right—fantasies like the Eastman bear stories were symptoms of a mind that couldn't deal with reality.

Well, she was dealing with reality the only way she knew how—she was leaving.

"Where are you off to?" the cabbie asked, making conversation.

"West," Susan replied, just now coming to a decision. "Out West."

Gone.

Disappeared.

Checked out of the hospital at eight in the morning and stepped into a cab. And from there...

Dean shook his head and put the four-carat diamond engagement ring back in its velvet box. He looked out the study window to the dull and lifeless courtyard, shrouded with a light fog that hadn't yet been burned off by sun.

In the last week, he had danced out on the courtyard, toasted his new love, laughed and made plans.

And had fallen in love.

And she was gone.

He didn't blame her, didn't feel the anger in his belly the way he had when Nicole left him. No, Dean knew the reasons that made Susan flee.

Funny, he knew her so well that he'd known she'd left as soon as he heard Dr. Sugar's voice on the phone that morning.

"We don't know where she went," Sugar had said.

"I'm sure she meant for it to be that way," Dean had replied.

She was so very much like him—tough and strong, proud and demanding of herself. With a smidgen too much pride that sometimes got in the way of living. Yet, in other ways, she was his polar opposite—quiet and conciliatory when he was inclined to be rash; sensitive and warm when he appeared to be brusque and clumsy with words and emotions. He wanted to win; she wanted to make peace. He demanded excellence in others; she marveled at all the ways a person was special.

He loved her, but he hadn't found the way to tell her so that she would believe him.

How could he have lived with her for so long and not noticed her until a bolt of lightning scrambled both their brains?

How could he have thought of her as no-nonsense, as dull, as simply a child-care worker.

Worse, how could he have driven her away?

For the first time in his life, he had failed.

He snapped shut the velvet jewelry box and dropped it on the desk.

Mrs. Witherspoon discreetly knocked on the open door.

"The Eastman people are here," she said. "I put them in the dining room and served coffee and croissants. They're waiting for you."

"I thought we were meeting at the office," Dean said.

"I changed that," Mrs. Witherspoon said briskly. "You don't look in any condition to drive downtown."

Dean frowned.

He followed her to the dining room and found seven somberly dressed executives seated at the table. All seven rose when Dean entered the room. Dean felt, rather than saw, his vice president in charge of finance take his place at Dean's side.

"Mr. Eastman," Dean said, holding out his hand to the elder president of the company.

"Mr. Radcliffe," the older man said with a nod.

After the introductions were made, Mrs. Witherspoon and Dean sat at the table. One of the Eastman executives coughed. Another nervously sorted through a sheaf of papers.

"We hope we are not here to listen to the terms of our death sentence," Mr. Eastman said mildly, breaking the tense silence.

Dean looked about the table. He saw himself through their eyes. The tough, merciless Dean Radcliffe. About to take their life's work and destroy it. They had no options because they were teetering on the brink of bankruptcy and no one else would help them.

He saw himself as they saw him, and then suddenly, he remembered how Susan saw him. How she looked within him to a tender heart that he had hidden for so long.

She believed in that tender heart.

She would always be with him—some part of her would. Even if the private investigator had this morning held out little hope that he could find her. Maybe she'd never be found, but until then, he could still act as if she were at his side.

"Gentlemen, let's talk reorganization," he said, taking from Mrs. Witherspoon a copy of the contract that he had drafted the week before.

He ripped the contract into two pieces and flung them down to the table like a challenge.

The executives stared at the paper.

Mr. Eastman looked up at Dean with his mouth open.

"Reorganization?" he asked.

"Yes," Dean said, feeling with every breath that he was closer to his Susan. Closer to her when he was the man she knew so well. He wanted to be that man. Even if he never saw her again, her mark upon him would be true and clear.

"Reorganization means…?" one of the younger Eastman executives asked.

"I've been talking with Mrs. Cohen, a toy store owner here in Winnetka who has a few ideas about your business," Dean said. "And I think we might like to implement them."

"Wait a minute," his vice president rasped. "I just got a list of bidders for the land. We were going to make a killing."

"You're exactly right," Dean said softly. "We were going to make a killing."

"Are you talking about a partnership?" one of the Eastman executives sputtered.

"Radcliffe Enterprises and Eastman Bears in partnership?" Mr. Eastman asked. "We thought we were meeting for an execution."

"A partnership," the executive seated at his right mused.

"Yes," Dean replied, suppressing the urge to smile at their obvious shock. "Now, Mrs. Witherspoon, could you organize some notes about our agreement this morning?"

She stared at him only briefly and then pulled out a steno pad.

"Certainly," she said.

"Let's develop a plan to make Eastman Bear Company the best teddy bear company in the country," Dean said to Mr. Eastman. "But I have one nonnegotiable item to put out on the table."

Mr. Eastman recoiled. The other executives set their jaws tightly.

Nonnegotiable.

That was the Dean Radcliffe they thought they knew—tough and uncompromising.

Whatever it was, it would be like a knife to the throat of the company. All the soft talk had been just that—talk.

"Yes?" Mr. Eastman asked warily.

"For every dollar by which we exceed last year's profit, we give twenty cents' worth of teddy bears to homes and charitable institutions that take care of needy and neglected children."

Mrs. Witherspoon gasped and dropped her pen on the table.

The executives stared at each other in disbelief, which gave way as they saw Dean's smile. A gambler's smile. A rogue's smile. The smile of a man who was having a little fun at business. And using his business to have some fun.

It was a smile none of them had seen before on Dean Radcliffe's face.

"It's all right, Mrs. Witherspoon," Dean said, noticing the tears welling up in her eyes. He followed her gaze to Mr. Eastman, whose own eyes softened.

Instantly Dean knew.

He knew why she had thrown such a fit about his purchase of the toy company.

His secretary and the president of Eastman Toys were in love.

Mrs. Witherspoon hardly seemed the type to fall in love, he thought, and then corrected himself.

Beneath all that cool efficiency, she was just an old softy at heart.

A lot of people are like that, Dean concluded.

Chapter Fifteen

Several months later, in a remote Wyoming town, Susan Graves struggled to put coats and boots on the eight preschoolers she cared for at the Faith, Hope and Charity Orphanage.

It was a difficult job but Susan loved it. She loved the little children she mothered, loved the orphanage, even loved the long hours—she fell into her bed in the upstairs dormitory each night so exhausted that she had no time for thinking about the past.

In fact, the only reminders of her unfortunate and silly episode at the Radcliffe home were two hand-drawn pictures she kept taped above her bed and a bracelet that held three very special charms. Other children had made her pictures, so Baby Edward's and Henry's drawings were crowded among the others. And the little charms on her bracelet got caught on things so often that Susan knew in her heart that one day, the bracelet might break apart.

But one thing she knew wouldn't change was her feelings for Dean. What he meant to her, what she felt about him, how he intruded on her heart. She loved Dean and always would. Every other part of her life was uncertain.

"Here, Eliza, put your foot in here," she directed. "And let me zip up the front. Tommy, put your boots on. John, we don't kick our friends."

"But he started it."

They always say that, she thought.

"Here. Let me help."

The voice came from behind her as she crouched down to zip up Eliza's snowsuit.

She had heard that voice so often in her head in the past few months.

But she had never heard it out loud.

Was she going crazy?

She turned around and looked up to him, standing over her.

She swallowed hard, and fell back on her hands, unsteady and overwhelmed. He crouched down next to her. He needed a shave, he looked a little beat, his white shirt was wrinkled, but otherwise, he was exactly as she remembered him.

"You're a tough woman to find," he said.

Susan stared at him openmouthed. Finally, she asked, "How did you find me?"

"I hired and then fired two private investigators," Dean answered, chuckling ruefully. "I endured several 'human interest' stories by Warber that were designed to generate publicity. I followed up every lead and was disappointed more times than I care to remember. But, in the end, this is what worked."

"What do you mean—'this'?"

"The Eastman Toy Company donates toys to needy children now. I deliver them when I'm free from business. I've got a pickup truck parked out back."

"You deliver toys?" Susan cried out. The concept of Dean Radcliffe in a pickup truck instead of his beloved Porsche, delivering toys to needy children instead of ultimatums to business competitors was simply and breathtakingly shocking.

"Sure," Dean said, as if his actions were the most natural thing for him to be doing. "I had no idea you were here. But I knew that if you love kids like I think you do, and if I'm handing out teddy bears to kids, I knew I'd find you one day."

"You...you handing out teddy bears?" Susan sputtered. "Dean Radcliffe, out of the boardroom and at the helm of a truck?"

"Yeah, call me Santa Claus. By the way, I'm

sorry about my appearance,'' he said. ''I've been on the road for over a week.''

''No need to apologize,'' Susan said, recovering her wits.

No apologies were necessary or warranted—Dean looked wonderful. The rumpled shirt and the five o'clock shadow saved him from the oh-so-perfect look that had been his trademark. He seemed more masculine, more at ease with himself and more of a man.

Oh, how she loved him. The months had done nothing to change that.

But what about him? What about his feelings? Had he fallen in love with a vision, creating a Susan in his mind who was as different from the reality as the woman who had been created by a stroke of lightning?

She enlisted his aid in getting the children's coats on and then asked one of the sisters to take the children to the playground. Then she led Dean into an empty conference room. He reached for her, but she eluded his embrace.

''The children miss you,'' he said.

''I miss them,'' she said cautiously, feeling the bracelet tugging at her wrist. She added neutrally, ''How are they doing?''

''Not well,'' he admitted. ''And I'm not, either. Susan, let me be blunt. Please come home.''

''I don't have a home, really,'' she said softly.

"You have one, but you're too damned proud to take it!"

Feeling boxed in by the way his frustration filled up the room, she started for the door.

He grabbed her arm, his actions first demanding and then pleading. Just like Dean.

"Susan, you said you're just like me, and you were right," he said, boldly challenging her with his eyes. "We're both proud and determined, and sometimes we shoot ourselves in the foot just to make our point. But we're lovers—even if we never made love. Susan, we're lovers, here, in our hearts. Nothing can change that."

"I'm not the woman you're in love with," she insisted.

"Oh, yes, you are!"

"Susan Graves?" she challenged skeptically.

"I admit I fell in love with someone a little flashier and a lot more sure of herself—and I didn't notice you much more than I'd notice a new dishwasher when you were the children's nanny."

"A dishwasher you would have noticed," she said dryly. "You didn't see me at all."

"But I've changed. And, like it or not, you've changed. You took risks when you were Susan Radcliffe. You were a great dancer. You were a fantastic hostess. And you were a wonderful kisser."

"That woman wasn't me."

"Then where did this come from?"

He leaned down and, with gentle nudges, drew her mouth up to meet his. She was reluctant, but her lips had pined for him so long that all her reasoning couldn't stop their opening to take him. His lips were tender and new, their kiss breaking up their reserves like the first tender shoots of spring. He enticed but didn't fully satisfy, and she knew that he wanted her acknowledgment, wanted her surrender.

His kiss was everything to her. And not nearly enough.

She shivered. He drew back.

"I don't know what you mean," Susan said. "I'm just me. Plain and simple and very ordinary Susan Graves. How could you ever fall in love with me?"

He laughed, the months of torment and worry now over. He had her, in his arms, his beloved.

"Susan, I don't think there's anything plain or simple or ordinary about you. Or about my love for you."

As she drew her head back from him, he saw the tears glittering on her cheeks like diamonds.

"You know, my next stop is a tiny little mission near Vegas," he said. "Come with me. A justice of the peace could make you Susan Radcliffe once and for all."

Fat raindrops began to hit the window. Susan looked out and saw the distant lightning on the underbelly of the clouds. It didn't fill her with fear, but with wonder and awe. The lightning didn't remind her of Wiley, or the shed, or the terrible blinding pain. The gentle lightning reminded her of candles. Of beautiful and delicate candlelight.

This was her moment, she knew.

Just like the candles on a birthday cake, this was her one chance to take her life's happiness. She could be proud, she could be reasonable, she could be sensible, she could be scared.

Or she could take a chance on having all her wishes fulfilled.

She had wished for happiness once.

Could she wish for it for the rest of her life?

"Will the justice of the peace make me Susan Radcliffe with or without a thunderbolt?" she challenged.

He let out a deep breath neither knew he had been holding.

"Baby, he'll just make you Mrs. Radcliffe. I'll provide all the excitement."

Chelsea, Baby Edward and Henry sat on the front porch of the Radcliffe home, waiting.

"She's coming home," Chelsea said, her voice a mixture of know-it-all-ness and a desperate worry that things might still not turn out right. She added, "Pretty soon now."

Henry peered down the path.

"I don't see anything. What if they get lost coming home? What if she changes her mind? What if...?"

"Oh, stop it," Chelsea said shortly. "She'll get here."

Baby Edward looked at each of them in turn.

"She'll come home because I wished it," he said.

"Well, we've all wished it," Chelsea said.

"But I wished it on Susan's birthday candles," Baby Edward insisted. "I didn't wish for toys—I wished for Susan to be with us forever."

"So did I!" Henry exclaimed.

And before Chelsea could tell him that she had wished the same thing, they saw their father's red pickup truck turn from the street onto the path.

"She's here!" they screamed in unison and tore down the front steps, their little legs pumping furiously.

The pickup stopped. The passenger door opened, and out stepped Susan. She crouched down and held her arms wide. Wide enough for all of them.

"Mom!" Chelsea cried.

She hugged them tight and then held Chelsea out so she could look at her.

"No," Susan said. "I'm Susan. Plain, ordinary Susan."

"Susan?" Chelsea said.

"Yes, Susan."

The children got into the flatbed and Susan took her place in the passenger seat. She looked at Dean and knew that she had finally found herself and the love that she was meant for. He smiled, put the truck in gear and drove the rest of the way to the house.

And that's how the not-at-all-plain, never-simple and by-no-means-ordinary, Mrs. Radcliffe came home.

* * * * *

Take 4 bestselling love stories FREE

Plus get a FREE surprise gift!

Special Limited-time Offer

Mail to Silhouette Reader Service™

3010 Walden Avenue
P.O. Box 1867
Buffalo, N.Y. 14240-1867

YES! Please send me 4 free Silhouette Romance™ novels and my free surprise gift. Then send me 6 brand-new novels every month, which I will receive months before they appear in bookstores. Bill me at the low price of $2.67 each plus 25¢ delivery and applicable sales tax, if any.* That's the complete price and a savings of over 10% off the cover prices—quite a bargain! I understand that accepting the books and gift places me under no obligation ever to buy any books. I can always return a shipment and cancel at any time. Even if I never buy another book from Silhouette, the 4 free books and the surprise gift are mine to keep forever.

215 BPA A3UT

Name	(PLEASE PRINT)	
Address	Apt. No.	
City	State	Zip

This offer is limited to one order per household and not valid to present Silhouette Romance™ subscribers. *Terms and prices are subject to change without notice. Sales tax applicable in N.Y.

USROM-696   ©1990 Harlequin Enterprises Limited

Wanted: Brides! This small South Dakota town needs women of marriageable age. And Silhouette Romance invites you to visit the handsome, extremely eligible men of:

a new miniseries by
Sandra Steffen

♥ The local veterinarian finds himself falling for his feisty receptionist—the one woman in town *not* interested in finding herself a husband.

LUKE'S WOULD-BE BRIDE
(June '97)

♥ This sheriff's got a reputation for being the good guy, yet a certain single gal has him wanting to prove just what a wolf in sheep's clothing he really is.

WYATT'S MOST WANTED WIFE
(August '97)

♥ A rugged rancher proposes a marriage of convenience to a dowdy diner waitress, but just wait till his ugly-duckling bride turns into a swan.

CLAYTON'S MADE-OVER MRS.
(October '97)

Don't miss any of these wonderful love stories, available only from

♥ Silhouette ROMANCE™

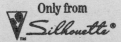

Bestselling author

JOAN JOHNSTON

continues her wildly popular miniseries with an
all-new, longer-length novel

The Virgin Groom
HAWK'S WAY

One minute, Mac Macready was a living legend in
Texas—every kid's idol, every man's envy, every
woman's fantasy. The next, his fiancée dumped him,
his career was hanging in the balance and his future
was looking mighty uncertain. Then there was the
matter of his scandalous secret, which didn't stand a
chance of staying a secret. So would he succumb to
Jewel Whitelaw's shocking proposal—or take cold
showers for the rest of the long, hot summer...?

Available August 1997
wherever Silhouette books are sold.

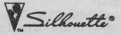

COMING NEXT MONTH

#1240 BABY BUSINESS—Laura Anthony
Bundles of Joy
Caring for infants was business as usual to lovely pediatrician
Tobie Avery, but when millionaire bachelor Clay Barton asked for
her help, Tobie wondered if the baby's rugged uncle would
consider her for a more permanent position—as his wife!

#1241 WYATT'S MOST WANTED WIFE—Sandra Steffen
Bachelor Gulch
Lisa Markman came to Jasper Gulch looking for a husband and a
new life. But Sheriff Wyatt McCully, a man with a reputation as
sterling as his badge, *wasn't* the man for her, no matter how sexy
or intriguing he was! Especially if the handsome lawman found
out about the past she was fleeing....

#1242 MARRY IN HASTE—Moyra Tarling
Jade had never forgotten the man who had pledged her his
heart, and then torn it away. Now devastatingly handsome
Evan Mathieson had returned, and was asking once again for her
hand in marriage. But could Jade trust their love a second time,
when she harbored a terrible secret that touched them both?

#1243 HUSBAND IN RED—Cara Colter
Sadie McGee was back home to care for her family. Romance
was *not* in her plans. But Michael O'Bryan, the town's golden
boy, had never forgotten the sexy girl from the wrong side of the
tracks—and would win her back no matter what....

#1244 THE RAINBOW BRIDE—Elizabeth Sites
A Western wedding? Pretty librarian Iris Merlin came to the old
town of Felicity looking for answers to her family's scandalous past,
not love! But rugged Adam Freemont soon captured her passion,
and had Iris dreaming of becoming the gorgeous man's wife.

#1245 MARRIAGE IS JUST THE BEGINNING—
**   Betty Jane Sanders**
To keep his little girl, single father Grant Parker would gladly marry
the lovely Sharon O'Riley—in name only. After all, Sharon had
known little Cassie since birth, and treated her as her own. But this
caring, warm beauty also had other charms, and Grant soon
suspected that marriage to Sharon was just the beginning....